CURSE OF THE GARGOYLES

GARGOYLE GUARDIAN CHRONICLES BOOK 2

REBECCA CHASTAIN

M
Y
M

www.rebeccachastain.com

Mind Your Muse Books
PO Box 374
Rocklin, CA 95677

ISBN: 978-0-9992385-2-3

ALSO BY REBECCA CHASTAIN

THE MADISON FOX ADVENTURES

A Fistful of Evil

A Fistful of Fire

A Fistful of Flirtation

A Fistful of Frost

Madison Fox Novella Box Set

NEVER MISS ANY NOVEL NEWS: Join Rebecca's newsletter today!

Visit RebeccaChastain.com

For all the fans who asked for another story about Mika and her gargoyles.

Thank you!

ACKNOWLEDGMENTS

This book would not exist without readers like you. When I originally wrote *Magic of the Gargoyles* (long before it was published), I never dreamed of turning it into a series. And then you guys liked it; you really liked it! Thank you for giving me a reason to spend more time in this fun world, and I hope you enjoyed it as much as I did.

For pointing out the problems in Elsa's motivations and the confusion of referencing Sleipnir (and more), thank you to my beta readers: Karl, Rebecca, Scott, Christina, Cathy, Maghon, and Kimberly. You guys are the best!

Carrie Andrews and Amanda Zeier, thank you for finding all the mistakes I glossed over a dozen times in my edits.

Noel, thank you for sharing your geology expertise and letting me pick your brain about rocks and minerals. Thanks to you, Mika doesn't sound like a Wikipedia version of an earth elemental.

For the amazing cover, thank you, Clarissa!

As always, Cody, the only thing that you could do to be a better, more supportive husband would be to find me a living gargoyle of my own.

Finally, thank you, Mom, for encouraging my love of reading as a child and continuing to champion all my stories. Your word today is *alula*, used in here just for you.

CONSTRUCTIVE ELEMENTS

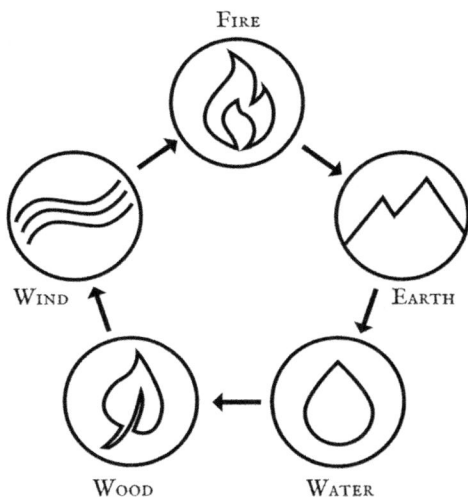

FIRE

WIND

EARTH

WOOD

WATER

DESTRUCTIVE ELEMENTS

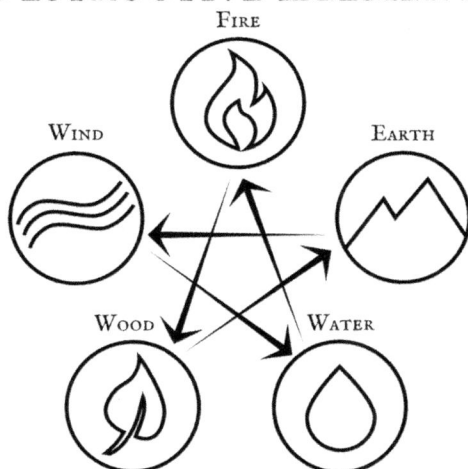

FIRE

WIND

EARTH

WOOD

WATER

1

ow's Oliver doing, Mika?" Kylie asked.

"H I jerked and glanced up from the journal open across my lap. We sat outside at a bustling café, soaking in the afternoon sun, and while I'd started out focused on double-checking my notes about my latest patient, a prasiolite and onyx gargoyle who had ingested moldy quartz loam, I'd long since stopped seeing the words. Instead, I'd been idly spinning a pentagram of the five elements above the pages, tuning them to perfect harmony with Oliver.

"Should I get another coffee?" Kylie asked, indicating her empty cup.

"Let me check." We'd been here a little over an hour. It was probably long enough.

I nudged the pentagram into flight, lifting it above the heads of people in the busy city pentagon before zeroing in on Oliver. The half-grown gargoyle crouched two buildings over and three stories up on his favorite perch on the peak of the library's marble facade, craning his long neck to peer over the edge to watch people come and go. Several government buildings and a few restaurants, including the café, ringed the pentagon, but Oliver preferred the magic of library users. I'd chosen the table where Kylie and I sat partially because it afforded me a view of Oliver at all times, but mostly because it was an outdoor seat close enough for me to reach him with my magic.

The pentagram kissed Oliver's side and dipped into his body. In the past five months, I'd perfected the elemental blend of my gargoyle companion: carnelian quartz earth, with a strong band of fire and smaller portions of wood, water, and air. I tried to be discreet and not disturb him, but he lifted his head to find me even as my magic told me he was feeling balanced and healthy.

"He's better now," I told Kylie. "Between an hour or two a week here and a couple hours at the market, he's stabilizing."

I let the weave dissolve and shut the journal. It'd been a gift from Kylie, and she'd had *Mika Stillwater, Gargoyle Healer* embossed in gold on the leather cover. After all these months, I still got the same nervous thrill at seeing my name and title together. Most of the time I still considered myself a midlevel earth elemental with a specialty in quartz—a specialty that happened to make me uniquely suited to work with the living quartz bodies of gargoyles. I loved my new career as a healer, but I kept expecting someone more powerful and knowledgeable to come along and replace me.

Standing, I hefted my bag filled with twenty-five pounds of seed crystals that I'd purchased earlier and wedged the journal on top before tightening the drawstring. Kylie deftly wove a basket out of air and levitated the cumbersome bag to knee height. I admired her skill. I could have created the same elemental lift, but I would have needed a boost of extra magic from Oliver to help me. I grabbed the over-the-shoulder straps and used them like a leash to keep the bag close to us as Kylie collected her research books and we exited the café.

"Do you think Oliver will stay behind this time?" Kylie asked.

"I doubt it." *He might if I encouraged him to.* I ignored the thought. "He's not like other gargoyles. He likes to wander."

"I think he just likes to be near you," Kylie said.

"Which is the problem." Gargoyles had a symbiotic relationship with humans. They could enhance our magic, making them coveted additions to any building or home. In turn, while they bolstered a person's magic, they also fed off it. Despite being made of stone, gargoyles required a balance of the elemental energies to be healthy. I suspected it was why most gravitated toward busy public buildings and the households of full spectrums, where the inhabitants all possessed powerful control over all five elements. Living with me, Oliver consumed mostly earth, and it threw his system out of whack, making him lethargic and potentially stunting his growth. As soon as I'd realized the problem, we'd started making frequent trips to public places where he could supplement his diet.

"It's not a problem," Kylie said. "You've figured out how to keep him healthy, and when he's with you, he's happy. Besides, look at it from his perspective. He's assisting Terra Haven's one and only gargoyle healer. I bet the other gargoyles are jealous."

"Ugh. That makes me sound disgustingly self-important."

Oliver released a trill loud enough to turn every head in

the busy pentagon, and the sound lifted my heart. He launched from the roof, startling a flock of pigeons when he unfurled enormous stone eagle's wings from his sinuous Chinese dragon body. Oliver was a glossy orange red of almost pure carnelian, from his square muzzle and stone beard to the feathery rock tufts at the tip of his long tail. With the sun shining through his rock feathers, he looked like he was suspended on wings of fire as he dove toward us. The graceful roll of his long body through the air made it easy to forget he weighed over a hundred pounds—until he landed too hard and his stone feet clapped against the cobblestones loud enough to echo through the surrounding buildings.

"Where are we going now?" Oliver asked. His voice had deepened as he'd grown, but it still carried the undercurrent of chimes and in no way sounded like it came from a stone throat.

Here was the moment to encourage Oliver to stay. With the variety of elementals who frequented the library, it would be a good, healthy home for him. But the words stacked up in my throat, and I swallowed them.

Oliver and his four siblings had been my first gargoyle healer case, and after I'd saved them, they'd stuck around to roost on the Victorian where Kylie and I both rented rooms. However, over the last few months, the other four had begun to explore various rooftops around the city, looking for more permanent homes. I kept waiting for Oliver to follow suit, all while hoping he'd stick around a little longer. Life without him was going to be lonely.

"To the gallery and then home. Unless you have some-where else to go, Kylie," I said. I'd been pointedly avoiding looking at Kylie so she wouldn't see my guilt, but I glanced her way when she didn't respond.

Kylie had stopped a few feet behind us, eyes riveted on a whirl of tangled air hurtling through a gap in the buildings and heading straight toward her. Though it moved fast enough to blur, I recognized her signature elemental twist on the bubble of captured sound: One of Kylie's rumor scouts had found something.

She pulled her white-blond hair aside as the air cupped her ear, feeding the message privately to her. Her blue eyes lit up and a flush brightened her pale cheeks.

"Well?" I asked. "What's the story?" If anything put that glow on my journalist friend's face, it was the possibility of a front-page piece of news.

"I don't know. Maybe nothing. I've got to go."

The weave dropped from beneath my bag and it crashed to the cobblestones, jerking my shoulder with it.

"Oh, sorry. Here." Kylie thrust her books into my arms. "I'll send word if I'll be done by dinner. Bye!" She spun and sprinted toward the nearest alley, shoulder-length hair streaming behind her as she disappeared around the corner.

"Okay, then. It's just you and me, Oliver." I crouched to add Kylie's books to my bag. This wasn't the first time Kylie had literally raced away, chasing a story. If it panned out, I'd find out about it tonight or tomorrow. In the meantime, I had errands to finish and work of my own. "Unless you want to stay," I forced myself to say.

"I want to see what sold," he said.

The tightness in my chest eased as I shared a smile with the little gargoyle.

I swung one strap of the bag over my shoulder and rested the awkward, poky bulk against my left hip, leaning to the right to compensate. After two steps, I switched sides with Oliver. His long body and four stubby legs gave him a bunching, loping gate, and his back kept bumping the bottom of the bag. Perhaps *little* wasn't the right term for him anymore. He was almost three feet long and half as tall with his wings closed. When he'd first come to live with me, he'd been small enough to hold. If I didn't stunt him and he kept growing at a normal rate, he'd reach over six feet long.

"Want to make any predictions?" I asked.

"The gargoyle pendants will be sold out, of course," he said. "Especially the ones of me."

"That goes without saying." My lifelong dream of becoming Terra Haven's preeminent quartz artisan had veered off course when I'd discovered I could heal gargoyles. Now, I wouldn't change a thing, but I still enjoyed working with inert quartz, and since being a gargoyle healer provided sporadic income, I made jewelry and sold the items through a local gallery to supplement my earnings.

"Maybe the wind current earrings, too," Oliver said, eyeing the earrings I wore. I wriggled my head to set the earrings in motion, and the gargoyle's bright eyes tracked the movement.

Like all my pieces, the earrings were made out of quartz. These were carnelian—at Oliver's request—and I'd reshaped the sturdy rock to slender, twisting ribbons so light the breeze fluttered them against my neck. Maintaining the structural integrity of the quartz while stretching it so thin took a level of skill that had taken me almost a decade to master. I owed my abilities as a gargoyle healer to those years of dedication, too. I'd worn my hair up so the sun could shine through the slivers of orange rock and catch people's eyes. Since I was the only person in the city escorted everywhere by a gargoyle, I tended to attract attention, and I wasn't above trading on the free advertising.

Oliver wriggled the ruff of rock fur behind his ears, as if

he were trying to mimic the movement of my earrings. Laughing at his antics, I completely missed seeing the bundle of elemental energy barreling toward me. The outer air layer hit me like a pillow upside the head, then bounced back and expanded into an oval sheet of fire held together with traces of air and water. Heat radiated from it, and I retreated a step when the golden and red flames reshaped into the perfect likeness of a man's face. He scowled, his bright eyes blazing straight into mine.

"Mika Stillwater," he snapped. "Your services are required on an urgent matter. Come at once."

Seeing the fiery face move was disconcerting enough; hearing the burning mouth bark my name chased a thrill of alarm down my spine. I clutched the handle of my bag tighter and shifted another step back. The disembodied flaming head followed.

I'd seen long-distance projections sent with such precision before, but only as invitations to special events. Given the tension in the man's face, he wasn't summoning me to a social gathering.

I opened my mouth to respond, but he looked to the side at something only he could see, then back at me. This time his gaze rested beyond my shoulder, and I realized it was a captured message, not a projection. I also realized I knew him.

"Your specialty is needed," he growled. The sphere collapsed into an arrow of pure flame. It darted away from me, then spun and pointed left down a side street. It held that position, quivering in place.

"Wasn't that—"

"Full-spectrum guard Velasquez," I said, finishing Oliver's question. *The most powerful fire elemental I'd ever met,* I added silently. You didn't make it into the ranks of the Federal Pentagon Defense, the country's most elite law enforcement organization, unless you were a full spectrum or nearly so. I'd had the good fortune to meet the local FPD full-five squad when I'd rescued Oliver and his siblings, but I hadn't expected to encounter the specialized team again, let alone receive a personal summons from the burly fire elemental.

Velasquez's words sank past my surprise. The only reason he would need me was if a gargoyle was in trouble.

"We need to hurry," I said, yanking my backpack's straps securely over both arms.

"Someone needs us!" Oliver shouted gleefully.

The moment I lurched into motion, the flaming arrow moved. As if attached to me by a stiff tether, it kept exactly the same distance between us even as I picked up my pace to a run. Oliver loped like an enormous inchworm ahead of me, his back arching and straightening with each stride, and he unfurled his wings for short glides to increase his speed.

Watching his increasingly long leaps, I was struck by a feeling of déjà vu. It'd been a race through the streets after a baby gargoyle that had altered the course of my life. Until that moment, I'd been a rather typical earth elemental, with a stable job and a life spent mostly behind a worktable. These days, I did a lot more rushing about, usually racing toward injured gargoyles, and I didn't think I'd ever get used to this nauseating jolt of adrenaline.

Between Oliver's stone feet pounding on the cobblestones, my heavy steps, and the clatter of seed crystals knocking together in my bag, we made enough racket to sound like a rampaging minotaur. People scurried out of our way and gawked from the edges of the road. Several waved and pointed, calling out encouragement. A few actually knew my name.

Our guiding arrow took us through downtown, winding along the least crowded roads. We pounded down wide sidewalks and through narrow alleys, and every time the arrow darted out of sight, I prayed it had stopped just around the corner so I could rest. My lungs and legs burned, and the heavy sack pummeled bruises into my lower back.

I zigzagged past a tavern and a haberdashery, before the narrow street opened into Focal Park. Or it should have. I stumbled to a halt. A massive blue-green ward twice as tall as the nearest building cordoned off the mile-long public park. As far as I could see up and down the street, emergency personnel held focal points of the shimmering ward at regular intervals. I braced my hands on my knees, sucking in oxygen. I'd never seen a ward that huge. It looked like it was designed to keep out an invading army.

And Velasquez's fiery arrow pointed straight at it.

———

A CROWD OF PEOPLE LOITERED OUTSIDE THE PARK'S EARTH entrance, where guards blockaded the pathway to a tunnel hidden behind the ward. Most of the people must have been herded from the park, judging by the number of blankets, picnic baskets, and various sports equipment they held. Questions rumbled through the displaced citizens, but I didn't hear any answers.

Together Oliver and I wormed through the crowd, and as people noticed Oliver, they cleared a path.

"Is there a sick gargoyle in the park?" someone shouted.

"I've heard gargoyles go berserk. Is that what happened?" another person asked.

I shook my head at the absurd question, but I couldn't take my eyes from the towering ward. What was Velasquez involving me in?

A woman burst through the crowd and grabbed my arm, and I yelped before recognizing Kylie.

"What's that?" she asked, pointing to the burning arrow hovering just this side of the ward. It'd received some nervous looks from the crowd and a few from the guards, too.

"Don't scare me like that," I said. "It's a summons from Velasquez." Kylie knew who the fire elemental was without me needing to remind her. She'd been there when the full-five squad had carted away the man who'd kidnapped Oliver and his siblings. Since then, she'd followed the squad more than once for a story. In fact . . . 'Was your rumor scout about the captain?"

Flushing, Kylie crossed her arms defensively. "Yes."

My stomach sank. Kylie had a standing rumor scout patrolling for mention of Captain Grant Monaghan, the air elemental in charge of Velasquez's squad. If the captain was here, the whole squad probably was, which meant the danger level was far greater than a sick gargoyle. The ward more than confirmed it.

"What did he say?" Kylie asked.

"He needs me."

Kylie's eyebrows shot upward. "That's what Mr. Gruffy-Pants himself said?"

"Basically." My footsteps had slowed while I talked, and Oliver butted my palm with a soft whine. The same urgency hummed in my veins, but I couldn't have Kylie following us into danger.

"Wait here," I told Kylie. "I'll tell you everything later.

It'll be an exclusive." I winked, then spun toward the tunnel entrance.

"Really? You thought that'd work?" Kylie fell into step on the other side of Oliver. "The people have a right to know what's going on in there, and if Grant is in there, I need to make sure he—ah, that the squad—is okay and . . . acting in the best interest of the citizens. A government that keeps secrets from the people is a corrupt government."

Her slipup was more telling than her ongoing protests about democracy and the balancing power of the press.

"Fine," I hissed as we approached the guards posted at the park entrance. The burning arrow hadn't moved from where it pressed an inch away from the ward, crushing my meager hope that Velasquez stood on this side of the ward.

"The park is closed," a tall woman in uniform said.

"I see that," I said, and Kylie snorted, then turned the sound into a cough. The guard scowled at us both. "I was summoned by FPD Fire Elemental Velasquez." I pointed to the arrow. "I'm a gargoyle healer, and he said I'm needed." I added a point toward Oliver, in case she'd missed the presence of the excited stone dragon who pranced between Kylie and me.

"And I'm her assistant," Kylie said. I wanted to protest, but I knew how much her career meant to her, and there was obviously a story on the other side of this magical curtain. Plus I was beginning to suspect her crush on Captain Monaghan might have developed into something more, so I kept my mouth shut and tried not to fidget.

The guard looped a bubble of air around the burning arrow and yanked it to us. She probed the elemental strands, and the message unfurled again. Velasquez's hard expression glared at the guard this time as he called me to his side without a single *please* or an ounce of deference in his tone.

When the message reverted to an arrow of flame, the guard released it and gestured for her companions to let us pass. Oliver trundled ahead with Kylie close beside him, but my footsteps lagged. As long as I remained on this side of the ward, I was safe.

But a gargoyle wasn't.

I hurried to catch up with Kylie and Oliver.

2

ylie stepped through the ward first, and I jumped to the side, startled, when threads of air anchored to her ears unraveled and slid down the smooth blue-green sheet of the ward, followed by a shimmer of fire and water from her linen shirt. The elements dissipated once they came untethered from her body and clothing.

"Hey!" Kylie protested, out of sight on the other side of the ward.

I pushed through the ward, and my scalp tingled, but otherwise I felt nothing more than a slight pressure.

"It took me ten minutes to perfect that antiwrinkle weave," Kylie complained, glaring at the ward with her hands on her hips. This close, the shimmery blue-green wall seemed to stretch all the way to the puffy white clouds. "No wonder I couldn't pick up any sounds from the park. This is criminal. The government keeping secrets from the public is reprehensible."

I patted my head. When I'd pulled my hair back in a ponytail, I'd wrapped my head in a twist of air to keep flyaways from escaping into a frizzy mess. The ward had sluiced the infinitesimal magic from me, which meant it was a two-way barrier. It was the kind of ward I'd expect in a holding cell at a guard station, not encasing the enormous public park.

I turned my back to the ward. A steep rocky bank rose in front of us with only a sliver of sky visible between the tunnel entrance and the ward. The long tunnel carved through the hill normally had plenty of ambient light reflected from both ends along a series of strategically placed mirrors, but with the ward blocking the sunlight on our side, the mouth of the tunnel gaped black and foreboding.

Oliver loped into the darkness, the echoes of his footsteps creating a dozen phantom gargoyles.

I grabbed fire energy, formed a small glowball, and followed him. Kylie trotted to catch up, sending three small glowballs ahead of us. When no monsters jumped out of the darkness, I stepped up my pace to a jog. Seed crystals and books battered my back.

"What was all that around your ear?" I asked Kylie.

"Trade secrets."

"They looked an awful lot like modified rumor scouts. How many ways do you have to spy on people?"

"Shh." Kylie glanced over her shoulder. The acoustics of the tunnel might have carried our voices to the guards on the other side of the ward if not for the cacophony Oliver created. Kylie must have come to the same conclusion, because she said, "Being a journalist is as much about finding a story as it is about writing it. How am I supposed to know where the stories are if I haven't got feelers in the field?"

"Feelers? Are you stalking more than Captain Monaghan?"

"I don't stalk anyone."

"Right. You're my assistant."

"Exactly." She beamed.

"In that case, help me out." I ducked out of the straps of my bag and thrust it toward Kylie. Since she had insisted on coming along, I didn't feel bad letting her take the burden. Not that it was a burden to her. With speed I envied, Kylie layered a net of air and settled the bag on top of it. Air was her element, and the bag floated obediently at her side without her having to hold the straps.

Oliver waited at the tunnel's exit, and I released my glowball when I caught up with him, squinting against the bright sunlight as I scanned the grounds. Somewhere ahead of us lay a danger great enough to ward off the park and call in the FPD. I didn't want to rush in blindly.

Oliver had no such caution and launched into the sky. I ducked aside to avoid the back draft from his wings and gathered a wad of raw magic. I had no idea what I'd do with it, but I felt better holding it.

A soft breeze fluttered my ponytail, pulling the coolness of the tunnel across the back of my neck. On any other warm, sunny day, the large granite boulders and tall rock plateaus dotting the sloped hill in front of us would have been crowded with sunbathers of every species.

"This is creepy," Kylie whispered.

I agreed. I scanned the horizon from our vantage at the top of the earth section, visually tracing the massive ward that could have wrapped thirty city blocks with room to spare. They'd even run the ward through Lincoln River to our left, where it edged the water section of the pentagon-shaped park.

Birds flitted through the canopy of a cluster of oaks nearby, chattering to themselves. A few squirrels scurried across the short grass. If it weren't for the lack of people and the daunting ward, I would have said nothing was wrong. No bolts of lightning pierced the sky. No horrors leapt from the rocks above us.

"What now?" I asked, stepping clear of the tunnel to check on Oliver.

A fiery arrow blossomed in the air a foot in front of me. I skittered backward and lashed out wildly with raw water and earth to counter the flames. My spastic defense missed the arrow by several feet and collapsed ineffectively on itself. The arrow floated down the hill, then froze in place, pointing the way.

A flush crept up my cheeks. We weren't under attack, and if we had been, my high-strung reaction would have been worthless.

"I guess we follow that," Kylie said, graciously not commenting on my bungled magic.

"Right." Not making eye contact, I jogged toward the arrow, unsurprised when it moved ahead of me on an invisible tether. I dodged tall pillars of rocks and leapt across the smaller gaps between the wide, smooth boulders. Without the burden of my heavy bag, I'd gotten my second wind and I practically flew down the slope. Kylie followed close on my heels, having no problem maintaining her air basket while running.

I scanned the park as I ran. The loudest sounds came from the right, where heavy reed wind chimes were scattered throughout the sculptures in the air section. The coal beds and shallow fire pits between the rock slope and air section were empty and quiet. Across the park, the botanical gardens twined up a slope above long grass sports fields. A small army could have hidden among the dense foliage and groves of trees, but only if they moved soundlessly.

The whole park naturally sloped to the left toward the streams and rowing ponds of the water section that fed into Lincoln River, but the arrow cut right, following a sand pathway that looped around the tiered rock gardens at the bottom of the earth section.

"I see them," Oliver shouted, diving haphazardly toward us. He flared his wings to cut his dive a few seconds too late and plowed furrows into the earth with all four feet. "They're in the center of the park. Hurry."

I pushed into a sprint. It'd taken us almost twenty minutes to reach the park. A lot could happen in that amount of time, especially to a sick gargoyle. Yet despite craning my neck to peer in every direction, I didn't see a cause for alarm, not even when I pounded up the slope to the heart of the park over a half mile from the tunnel and found the entire full-five squad.

The center of the park mirrored the outer boundaries in a smaller pentagon, this one marble, with a pentagram etched into it and the deep grooves coated with smooth glass. Centered on a ten-foot-tall plateau and ringed in sycamore trees and pillars of granite, the pentagram was used in elaborate and powerful spells, and I expected to find the captain and his squad arrayed at their respective focal points, deep in some massive weave of magic, fighting a colossal and scary enemy. Instead, they clustered to the side around a gargoyle standing in the shade of a sycamore.

Clutching a cramp in my side, I trotted across the pentagram toward the gargoyle. He stood frozen, elemental magic swirling around him, and a flashback to finding Oliver and his siblings paralyzed in life-draining traps jolted fresh alarm through me. A complex shield swirled around the trap, but someone blocked my line of sight before I could see more. Blinking, I took in the whole scene.

I didn't know anyone's first name but Captain Monaghan's—thanks to Kylie's obsession with him—but I remembered all their faces. Marciano loomed a head taller than everyone else, close to seven feet tall, as if his body had grown to mimic the trees of his element. He stood next to a slender redhead, the water elemental Winnigan, and they maintained the shield I'd caught a glimpse of. The captain had shifted closer to Seradon to study something she pointed to, and it was his broad chest and shoulders blocking my view. The man was intimidatingly large, which I supposed was useful in his profession, if aggravating right now. I might have mistaken the sturdy earth elemental beside him for a man, with her short brown hair and tall, muscled body, but next to the captain, Seradon almost looked petite.

"We're going to have to do this without her," the captain said. "We can't wait any longer."

"She's here." Velasquez stood a little apart, arms crossed over his thick chest. Everyone in the squad was in prime physical condition, but he looked like he could pick up the full-grown gargoyle in front of them and not break a sweat. His dark blue eyes shifted to track Oliver, who had veered wide around the pentagram and then rushed to the shielded gargoyle. Velasquez stepped in front of the charging stone dragon, and Oliver scrambled to stop without crashing into him, flapping his wings to counter his forward momentum.

I didn't hear what Velasquez said to Oliver because the captain and Seradon had turned to face me, and the weight of their combined gazes slowed my steps.

"Perfect timing," Seradon said with a friendly smile.

Velasquez's guiding arrow dove toward the shielded

gargoyle. It flared wide and bubbled into a solid ball of flame, expanding in a flash. Seradon ducked to avoid being engulfed. Velasquez grabbed the wildly pulsing magic and slashed it apart. The arrow winked out of existence with a puff of smoke.

"Yep, not a moment too soon," Seradon said.

I stared. That wasn't how magic worked. A weave didn't morph into something else, and it didn't expand without added fuel.

"What's going on?" I asked.

"See for yourself," Seradon said, gesturing for me to examine the gargoyle.

I checked his face first, and his lifeless eyes ratcheted my tension.

That's just how gargoyles' eyes look when they're unconscious, I reminded myself, taking no comfort from the thought.

He had the body of an earthy brown jasper marmot, though far larger than the mammal counterpart ever grew. Standing on his back feet, he nearly looked me in the eye, and the reindeer antlers arching from behind his little ears stretched two feet above my head. Enormous wings draped his back, falling to curve against the earth behind his feet. Blue dumortierite tipped his feathers and antlers.

I paced around him, checking his body visually when all I wanted to do was get my magic into him. At one time, he'd been beautiful, but now pockmarks and erosion marred his hide, a sign of poor nutrition. Terra Haven had no shortage of the quartz loam all gargoyles needed in addition to a steady diet of magic, but something had prevented this gargoyle from getting a good meal.

I suspected it was the massive contraption encasing him. The shield warped the view, but I could make out oblong

loops of wicker, metal, glass, alabaster—and feathers?—
evenly spaced around the gargoyle and pressed so tightly to
the length of his body that they bent and met above his
head. Elements twisted along the loops and filled the empty
space, but the ward distorted the details.

"Who let *you* in here?" Captain Monaghan barked, and I
jumped. The imposing air elemental wasn't looking at me,
though.

Kylie planted her hands on her hips and lifted her chin.
She stood a head shorter than the captain, but she made it
seem like they looked eye to eye. "The constitution."

Grant snorted. "You're stalking me."

"Wow. Carting around that massive ego must be a
burden."

"How did you know where to find me?"

"Must have been the flaming arrow."

Grant narrowed his dark brown eyes, his face a thundercloud. I'd have taken a step back, but Kylie dismissed him,
turning to face the gargoyle.

"How long's this . . . thing been on the gargoyle?" She
leaned close to the shield, squinting at the magic flowing
inside.

Grant grabbed her by her elbows, lifted her off her feet,
and deposited her several paces behind us next to a
slouched woman I hadn't noticed. "Stay here. Don't inter-
rupt," he ordered.

Kylie's eyes bulged and she opened her mouth, but
Grant had already turned away. She settled for crossing her
arms and glaring at his back for all of a second before
crouching beside the woman. The stranger slouched with
her elbows on her bent knees and her head in her hands,
rocking herself. Long black hair hid her face, and she
flinched when Kylie touched her arm.

"I still say Mika shouldn't be here," Marciano said, his deep voice a gentle rumble. He didn't look away from the shield when he spoke. "She's going to get hurt."

"This is going to require a delicate touch, especially for the gargoyle," Seradon said. She watched the captain instead of the wood elemental. "Mika's a gargoyle healer and she has incredible strength in her specialty with quartz. You've seen her work. She can do things I can't. We need her."

In desperation, I'd once created a trap spun like a web through hundreds of pieces of quartz. My life and the lives of five gargoyles had depended on making the trap hold until the FPD arrived, so I'd put everything I had into it. Seradon had been impressed with my use of quartz—more so than I realized.

"That was a one-time thing," I said. "I haven't done anything that complex since."

"Well, you're about to. That damn contraption is fused to the gargoyle."

Fused? I bent to get a better view. There, on the gargoyle's neck, a rod of quartz had been grafted into the jasper fur, and both ends of the metal loop fed into the quartz. I watched, horrified, as a surge of raw elemental magic speared into the gargoyle, then retracted twice as strong, flowing through the quartz implant and circling the metal loop.

No wonder the gargoyle looked so terrible: The bizarre contraption was sucking out his life!

I pushed closer, only to be brought up short by Velasquez. He'd grabbed my bicep in an iron fist, preventing me from smacking into the squad's shield.

"Careful," he said.

"What are you waiting for?" When Velasquez didn't

answer me, I spun to face the captain, breaking the fire elemental's grip on my arm. "We need to get that . . . that *thing* off the gargoyle."

"You need to understand what we're working against," Seradon said. "Elsa calls it a 'purifier.'"

"Elsa?"

Seradon glanced at the dark-haired woman on the ground. She'd stopped rocking and was talking quietly with Kylie. "It's supposed to separate the elements into their purest forms," Seradon continued. "It's her grand plan to manually create the magical enhancement of a gargoyle."

"That's impossible." Gargoyles were unique in their ability to enhance magic in others. With a boost from a gargoyle, a person could more than double the amount of magic they could wield. No artificial source or man-made contraption could replicate it. "Even if it were possible, what's it doing *feeding* off this gargoyle?"

"It turns out that to mimic a gargoyle's enhancement, she needed a gargoyle as a power source."

Before I could ask why Elsa wasn't in null bands and on her way to the nearest guard station, Seradon continued.

"If that wasn't bad enough, her idea of 'purifying' the elements is to rip them apart—polarize them into segregated sections—to make each stronger."

"What do you mean?" No matter the strength, the elements always coexisted.

"Look here. And here." Velasquez gestured around the gargoyle. "The *purifier*"—he spat the word—"isn't letting the elements touch inside the loops."

I stared at the end of the wicker loop as it sucked a pulse of magic from the gargoyle, draining its life one surge at a time. My fists clenched. Dragging my gaze from the horrific implant, I squinted at the space between the wicker and feather loops. Now that I knew what to look for beneath the elements in the ward, it didn't take me long to make out the raw wood energy eddying in complete isolation. I checked the space between the feather and glass loops. A funnel of air whipped through the tight space and buffeted the inside of Marciano and Winnigan's shield.

The polarized magic, as Seradon had labeled it, shouldn't have remained confined in between the segregated sections. The looping objects hooked into the gargoyle weren't solid; they were fragile-looking bands. Yet the magic reacted to them as if they were impenetrable walls. The only logic the two sections of the contraption followed was the most basic one: wood fed air. Every time a fresh surge of magic siphoned from the gargoyle to feed the wood section, the pocket of pure air also grew stronger, proving some interaction occurred between the two sections.

I moved with Velasquez, circling the gargoyle. Oliver paced at my heels, a low rumbling sound close to a growl vibrating in his throat. The pattern repeated all the way around the trapped gargoyle. The polarized elements each fed the next in a constructive cycle: wood strengthening air, air strengthening fire, fire strengthening earth, earth strengthening water, and water strengthening wood. The diabolical design ensured that the magic bled from the gargoyle perpetually strengthened the purifier.

As if having his life stolen in torturous increments wasn't enough, being bombarded by the divided magic had to be wrecking the gargoyle's internal systems. No wonder he was unconscious.

"How long has the gargoyle been trapped?" I asked. Judging by the pockmarks along his body, I'd have guessed months, but someone would have noticed the purifier at work long before now if that were the case. If it could do this much damage in a few minutes or hours, we were wasting precious seconds.

With a choked cry, Kylie stumbled back from Elsa and caught herself against a granite column. "She's got no magic," she blurted out. "I think Elsa is fried."

"Probably for life," Velasquez agreed. No sympathy registered in his tone.

A chill ran down my arms. Being able to see the elements and not touch them, to never again be able to use magic—I'd rather be dead than burned out.

"From what we can tell, she did it to herself when she hammered the last quartz nail into the gargoyle and activated it," Seradon said, her voice as flat as Velasquez's. "We were contacted when a concerned citizen saw the magic backlash."

Crap. This purifier was more dangerous than it looked, and it looked plenty sinister. "What are you waiting for? Free the gargoyle so I can get to work."

"That's the problem," Seradon said. "I can't remove the purifier without killing the gargoyle. I need you to do it."

"Me?" I squeaked. The last person who had worked on this contraption had been nullified. *Probably for life.* What made Seradon think I could succeed where she couldn't? She was an FPD squad member and a full spectrum, strong in earth *and* the other four elements. I was a gargoyle healer, a midlevel earth elemental at best. "I can heal the gargoyle once he's free"—I hoped—"but destroy this? I couldn't."

Oliver whined and brushed his cool, glass-smooth head against my palm. I swallowed hard.

"Next to Seradon, you're the person with the best chance," Velasquez said.

Startled, I met his gaze. I hadn't expected encouragement, however paltry, from the stoic fire elemental.

"You wouldn't be dismantling it all on your own, either, only the parts connected to the gargoyle," Seradon said.

What else was there? Once the purifier wasn't feeding on the gargoyle, it should collapse. If it were only a matter of removing the quartz from the gargoyle, I wouldn't hesitate. But I didn't need to see the weave around the loops to know it was far more complex than anything I'd encountered before.

"If she doesn't feel like she can do it, she shouldn't," the captain said. "One trick doesn't make her a quartz savant. The last thing this quake-storm needs is a rookie with limited pentacle potential and questionable linking skills."

"Hey!" Kylie protested. "Mika can do this." She marched into Grant's personal space, as if she could convince him through intimidation—as if she could intimidate him at all. "She's a *gargoyle healer*. It's in her blood."

The captain's shot at my limited elemental abilities stung my pride. I'd spent a lifetime perfecting my skills with quartz to prove I could compete with full spectrums in my field, and I'd done it. I could manipulate and refine quartz into creations so delicate they looked like spun sugar. I could heal the complex living quartz systems of gargoyles.

But spinning quartz or patching a gargoyle was a long way from practicing combat magic against a powerful weave that had nullified its creator, especially with a gargoyle's life on the line.

Seradon ignored Kylie's outburst and spoke to me. "This monstrosity is dangerous and getting more so—"

"Definitely getting more so," Winnigan said, her voice strained.

"Dormant or not, the gargoyle can't withstand much more of this," Seradon continued. "I'll back you up, but you should lead the magic. You're the healer."

"She said no," Grant said, turning away from Kylie's glare.

"She's scared," Velasquez said.

I broke my stare with the gargoyle's dead eyes to look at him. He held my gaze while continuing to speak as if I couldn't hear him. "Give her a second to warm up her courage."

He winked.

I blinked and looked away. Fear clogged my throat. *Nullified.* No healer had ever cured nullification. If I tried and failed, my ability to use magic could be permanently amputated.

"Captain, I need to be free to help with the shield," Seradon said. "If this thing unravels—"

"No. No," Elsa moaned, rocking faster. Kylie took a step toward her but stopped when Elsa looked up. Tears streaked the inventor's face, and her eyes darted wildly and unfocused.

"You're wrong! You're all wrong." Elsa burst to her feet and rushed the captain. He thrust Kylie behind him before catching the wild-eyed inventor and holding her at arm's length.

I touched Kylie's arm and pulled her farther to safety.

"If I could just..." Elsa wiggled her fingers, then clenched them into fists when nothing happened. Contempt twisted her features. "You're useless. You're all *useless*! Full spectrums don't deserve the power they have. They don't deserve to be the only people gargoyles favor. Power should be distributed by intelligence, not birth and not based on the decision of an *animal* with a rock for a brain. My purifier was going to fix it all and you'd have nothing to be so sparking *arrogant* about." Elsa included me in her scathing look, lumping me in with the FPD squad. "Can't you idiots see? You're wasting time. You can't contain it. You have to crush it. Now, before it kills us all. I tried. But I . . . but I . . ." Elsa wiggled her fingers again and a laugh more sob than mirth crumpled her.

The captain released her, his face a study of neutrality. "Someone needs to get her out of here."

"You can do this, Mika," Kylie whispered. "This gargoyle needs you."

Doubt ate at my stomach lining even as I longed to help the stone-still gargoyle. He had to be under enormous strain, and the longer we talked, the worse he faired.

"If we suppress the magic while that invention is embedded in the gargoyle, he'll die," Seradon said, shaking her head. "We can't—"

"You can. *You have to.*" Elsa clutched the front of Grant's uniform, her eyes feverish. She might have tried to shake him, but he didn't budge. "It's ripping the elements apart— it'll rip apart the city—and the gargoyle is the problem. I wouldn't be . . . be . . . I would be whole if the gargoyle wasn't broken. It's not moderating its boost. You have to snuff out the gargoyle to break the purifier or we'll all die."

Broken. Not *sick.* Not *injured.* Broken. Like the gargoyle was a tool, not a living creature.

Fury bubbled through my blood. I didn't know how Elsa had convinced or trapped the gargoyle into her horrifying machine, but it was clear she saw him only as a means to an end. It was the curse of gargoyles: Their giving nature made them the targets of greedy people who had no qualms about using and abusing them for a nonconsensual magic boost. That Elsa had tortured the gargoyle in her quest to mimic his ability to enhance magic only made it worse. She wanted to steal one of the facets of his very nature, and she thought nothing of killing him in the process.

Grant pried Elsa's fingers from his shirt and I shoved in between them, pushing Elsa back with my wrath.

"You created this disaster. You drilled your experiment into the *flesh* of a living creature, and you're blaming the *gargoyle*? You deserve to be nullified."

I spat my final words at the cowering woman and listened to them fade in the ensuing silence.

"They're gone. They're all gone," Elsa moaned. Her tears morphed into full-body sobs and she crumpled to the ground. I turned away.

Oliver reared up on his hind legs, flaring his wings and hissing at Elsa. I patted his head.

"We're not letting this gargoyle die because she's afraid." *Or because I am.*

Anger helped counter some of my fear. The gargoyles needed someone they could depend on to help them. I'd been passing myself off as a gargoyle healer; I couldn't turn aside now when things got dangerous. If Seradon thought I had a better chance of saving the marmot's life than she did, I had to try.

I looked up, expecting censure. Grant, Seradon, and Velasquez watched me approvingly. Kylie had her "I told you so" expression firmly in place when she met Grant's eyes.

"See? She got her courage all warmed up," Velasquez said.

3

"Okay. We'll let Mika give it a try," Grant said.

"Excellent idea, sir," Seradon said, earning a flat look from the captain.

I fisted the hem of my shirt in my shaking fingers to hide them. This was the right decision. I might not be the strongest elemental, but I was strong where it mattered. I was a gargoyle healer.

For now. If I get burned out, I won't be healing anyone, my traitorous subconscious whispered.

"Get up," the captain said, half lifting Elsa to her feet. He bound her hands behind her back with tight null bands. The spell in the ropes was redundant, but they still functioned as strong restraints. Elsa slumped forward, her long dark hair hanging in curtains on either side of her face. "Kylie Grayson, you will escort Elsa to the ward. I want her in the custody of the city guards."

"But—"

"And you *will* stay on the other side of the ward," Grant said, the full command of an FPD captain in his tone. "I'm not taking the chance of you distracting Mika."

Kylie's spine snapped straight, but rather than argue, she looked to me. I read the question in her expression: If I wanted her to, she'd go against Grant's orders and remain. I shook my head. As wonderful as it'd be to have her supportive presence, she wouldn't be able to do anything. I'd breathe easier knowing she was safe on the other side of the massive ward.

"Fine. Good luck, Mika." Kylie gave Oliver a quick pat and whispered something to him, then reached for Elsa.

"You're letting me go?" Elsa asked, bewildered.

"You're under arrest, but you can't stay here."

"Thank the gods." She fled. With her arms imprisoned behind her back, Elsa couldn't balance well, but that didn't slow her down. Kylie scrambled to catch up.

A fresh wave of icy trepidation slid down my body.

"Don't even think about spying," Grant called after Kylie. "No listening weaves are going to penetrate that ward."

"You know, this *is* kind of scary," Velasquez said to me. He peered at the divided magic inside the shield. "She was right. If the purifier gets loose, it'll rearrange the very laws of magic itself."

I glanced at his expression. His tone was matter-of-fact, without a hint of the terror his words evoked in me. Like the others in the squad, he looked focused, as if this level of danger was an everyday challenge. Maybe for them it was.

"You'll need to link with us—to get through our shield and for your safety," Seradon said.

Velasquez shifted to my left and Grant took a position to Seradon's right. Marciano and Winnigan moved so the squad was evenly spaced around the shield and gargoyle. Oliver launched into the air, flapping heavily to the rock pillar behind Grant where he could oversee everything. I glanced back the way Kylie had departed. She and Elsa were out of sight. In the enormous park, it was just the full-five squad, one half-grown gargoyle, a trapped gargoyle, and a very out-of-place midlevel earth elemental.

"Have you ever linked with five full spectrums before?" Seradon asked.

"No." Powerful people didn't tend to include midlevel people like me in their group spells.

"There's nothing special to it." Seradon squared off in front of me and I had to look up to meet her brown eyes. She smiled encouragingly, but I didn't try to smile back—fear had frozen my features. "Just like any other link, open yourself to equal parts of every element, then feed it to me. I'll pull you into the link and help you stabilize yourself."

"Okay." It sounded simple. I gathered earth, air, fire, wood, and water in equal amounts. My ability to manipulate air and water was limited, not even midlevel, which meant I barely held any wood, earth, and fire when I matched up their levels. I eased this thimble of power into Seradon, fidgeting with embarrassment. Seradon's stream of elemental energy merged into mine, linking us with a subtle hook.

"Good. Smooth," Seradon murmured.

The world dropped open inside me as magic flooded into me. I'd expected the link to feel like a gargoyle's enhancement. Their natural boost increased my own elemental strengths, giving me access to more magic, but this was so much more.

Five magical signatures pressed against the periphery of my awareness, but I couldn't pinpoint an individual. The link also had shape and intent. Elemental layers wrapped and wove through each other to create the shield, and I could see every strand and how it had been assembled. The purifier beat against the underside of the shield, and in noticing the tension in the shield, I became aware of the strain in the link. Holding the shield taxed the squad—or some of them. I couldn't tell if it was only Winnigan and Marciano becoming fatigued or all of them.

Magic blossomed anew inside me, and I recognized it this time. Oliver had joined us, enhancing the magic in our link. Awed by the amount of power available to me, it wasn't until Seradon gripped my elbow that I remembered I had a body. Oliver trilled, and I rediscovered my hearing. The young gargoyle's carnelian eyes glowed like small suns, and with his wings flared and his posture flexed with his intent focus, he looked majestic. Through the link, he cycled more magic than he'd access if he spent a week atop the library. If he hadn't been balanced earlier, he would be after this.

"It's disorienting the first time," Seradon said. I pivoted to look at her, and the park blurred in my vision. Inside the link, someone poured water into the cracks in the shield, shoring up weak points. Magic moved through me—pulled through me—without me using it, and the sensation spiraled my focus inward.

"I'd like to give you more time to get adjusted, but we need to work fast."

I nodded to show I understood, then closed my eyes when the horizon moved with my head.

"I'm going to pull you through the shield," the earth elemental continued. She'd taken my hand at some point, and her fingers tightened on mine. I squeezed back.

Somehow, Seradon collected *me* from the linked energy. With a feeling like she tugged the elements through me, she gathered my contribution and dipped it through the shield.

"I'll use the purifier's pathway to get us to the gargoyle," Seradon said. "Then it's up to you once we reach the quartz."

I opened my eyes and squinted at the purifier. I could feel myself—or rather, my magic—resting on the underside of the shield, buffeted by the pounding pressure of the polarized water element, but the sensation was distant. Seradon was buffering me.

She had aligned us with a thin metal strip defining the line between the polarized water and earth elements, and I got my first good look at the complexity of the purifier. A tangle of helixes so dense they looked braided spiraled around the metal, each made of one strand of earth and one strand of water. Hundreds of tiny fingers of earth connected each helix, all of them feeding magic from the polarized earth section into the strands of water, strengthening them. In turn, the water strands spun pure water into the polarized section on the left.

I'd never seen anything like it, especially not the way the helixes cascaded down the empty center of the metal loop, maintaining a perfect wall between the two polarized elements. On the left, the spinning water strands kept the water from flowing back into the earth section. On the right, the earth strands absorbed energy from the polarized earth section and fed it through the helixes into the water.

Seradon used a scissor of air and wood to sever the helixes atop the metal and provide a clear path for us. Raw water element battered her weaves from one side, earth on the other, but they couldn't counter her destructive magic, not on the scale she wielded through the link. Faster than I would have thought possible, she tore apart the magic surrounding the thin metal and unplugged it from quartz.

Success! If we could break through all the loops and the magic that wrapped them as easily, we could take the power out of this contraption in no time.

It almost seemed like the marmot was helping or

fighting back, too. A thin inner bubble of normal, coexisting elements rested between the gargoyle's pockmarked skin and the polarized energy.

Behind us, the helixes divided and duplicated, reweaving a tangled braid along the metal. Before today, I would have said with complete conviction that the elements required a person or creature to shape them into a pattern. Destroyed weaves dissipated; they didn't reconstruct a previous pattern—only this one just had.

"How is that possible?"

"Elsa might be able to explain it," Seradon said. "All I need to know is it rebuilds itself and it's faster than the five of us could counter, thanks to the fuel source of the gargoyle. That's partly why we need to disconnect it."

Of course. If it had been easy, the squad would have taken care of the problem already.

"Your turn," she said. "Cut off the purifier from the gargoyle, and we'll deal with the rest."

She made it sound almost easy.

I gathered a balance of elements, and magic swamped me, feeding from five incredibly powerful people and enhanced by Oliver. Flailing, I fought for control.

"Relax," Seradon said. "Let it go and try again."

With a gasp, I released the elements. Instantly, I was back to being a part of the link, not drowning in it. I took a deep breath, then teased a minuscule balance of elements from the link. A rush of magic responded, nearly as much as I could wield when enhanced by a gargoyle but still a manageable amount.

I probed the quartz implant. Elsa had drilled the ragged, two-inch hole with a blade of elemental wood, then wedged a sharp quartz crystal into the wound, fusing the rock to the gargoyle's muscles and flesh with crude bridges of earth.

She hadn't even tuned the earth element to quartz, let alone to the more specific resonance of the gargoyle's jasper body. She'd anchored her doomed purifier to the gargoyle the way a person might pound stakes of a tent into the ground, as if the gargoyle had no more feeling than the soil. I gritted my teeth. Being nullified was too good a fate for Elsa.

I tuned my elemental bundle to resonate with the gargoyle by rote, narrowed the amount I held to a gentle stream, and slid a feeler into the marmot.

Ice-hard water blocked me, and my magic cut into the gargoyle when it should have penetrated painlessly. Grabbing more water, I matched my feeler to the unbalanced energies in the marmot. Pulses of pain, steady as a heartbeat, pounded into my brain through my connection to the gargoyle. I didn't have to open my eyes to know the pain strobed in rhythm with the purifier's energy as it drove polarized elements into the gargoyle and sucked out raw, enhancing magic.

I slid deeper into the gargoyle, then scrambled to reconfigure the elements I held to balance with the marmot, pulling in more wood and letting go of a lot of earth. This wasn't natural. A gargoyle should be the same resonance throughout. When I realized what it meant, my eyes popped open.

"He's polarizing on the inside," I said.

Seradon's sympathetic brown eyes slid from the gargoyle to me. "I know."

"I don't feel him fighting back. I thought he was because he's kept the magic near his skin normal, but inside it's like he's . . ." *Dead.* I didn't want to say it out loud, not within the marmot's hearing.

"While he's dormant, I don't think he can fight."

"How did Elsa do this to him?"

"Greed makes people do horrible things."

That wasn't what I meant. I wanted to know how she'd made the gargoyle "dormant" in the first place, but now wasn't the time for a drawn-out conversation. The gargoyle felt fragile. The divided energy was eroding his innards, and if he took much more abuse, he'd be torn apart from the inside out in a cruel and agonizingly slow death.

Taking a deep breath, I closed my eyes and retracted my elemental feeler from the gargoyle back to the quartz implant. It was time to prove myself worthy of my title.

I couldn't disconnect the thick bands of earth element welding the quartz to the gargoyle without hurting him, so I opted for quick slices of wood.

Magic oozed from the fresh cuts, and tendrils of helixes stretched toward the fresh wounds like magical leeches. I hacked them away and layered patches across the cuts, tuning my magic to the marmot's current balance on the inside and to strong jasper quartz on the outside, effectively sealing the cuts.

I would have preferred to use the crystal to pack the wound, reshaping it as I might a seed crystal into quartz the marmot's body could eventually absorb, but the impurities in the crystal made that impossible. If I'd been able to reach it, I would have extracted the foreign quartz with my fingers, but since the shield and purifier wouldn't let me physically close to the gargoyle, I had to remove it using the elements. I considered a burst of air to push it from the open wound, but I didn't want to cause the gargoyle additional pain from the backlash of pressure. I also didn't have time for any finesse. I grabbed the quartz crystal where it was attached to the metal loop of the purifier and reshaped the rock into a blunt knob too large to fit back into the gargoyle's wound.

I was admiring my handiwork when the purifier's weave

reknit around the quartz and arced from the knob into the hole drilled into the gargoyle's neck. Raw magic pulsed out of the gargoyle through quartz embedded on the other side of his neck.

"No!" I sliced through the purifier's weave, tearing it apart all the way around the metal loop. The moment I stopped, the weave started to regrow. I switched strategies and attacked the wall of helixes suspended inside the loop. My blades of air and wood sliced a path from the top of the metal circle to the bottom, severing a thousand complex looping strands between the polarized water and earth sections.

The weave should have dissolved. The influx of earth flowing into water through the gap I'd created should have shattered the rest of the elemental wall. Instead, the barrier grew back together into the same pattern as before, and watching the magic rebuild itself made my skin crawl.

"You're making it worse. Concentrate on the gargoyle, Healer," Seradon said.

I jerked my attention back to the gargoyle, heart sinking to find him weaker. I severed the purifier's connection with the gargoyle again and grabbed the quartz knob, flattening it against the metal. It wasn't enough; the pathway was established, making the quartz redundant, and the purifier's weave jumped the gap again. I needed a blockade.

Hoping I could count on the purifier to behave like normal elemental magic, I formed a destructive pentagram, layering the elements to counter each other. I wedged the pentagram into the reshaped quartz and bound it in place with ties of quartz-tuned earth. When the purifier's weave hit the quartz this time, it burrowed into the pentagram, shredding it. Without the presence of all five elements to balance the pentagram, it couldn't withstand the influx of earth and water. I reshaped it, stronger this time in wood and air to counter the disproportional elements; then I grabbed the center of the pentagram and inverted the elements. I'd never tried such a complex maneuver before, yet with the strength of the squad behind my weaves, it was almost easy.

The purifier's energy fell through the center of the pentagram, then curved back to spin through the destructive elements embedded in the quartz. The affluence of energy reinforced the barricade, cycling through the pentagram in a nonstop five-pronged loop that prevented it from jumping the hairbreadth of space between the metal rod and the gargoyle's punctured neck.

"Good thinking. I wouldn't have considered using the quartz like that."

Seradon's voice floated across my consciousness but didn't fully register as I raced for the next quartz implant. With righteous fury, I severed the purifier's weave—this time wood and water from a wicker loop—then sliced through the clumsy earth elements grafting the quartz to the gargoyle. In seconds, I'd flattened the quartz onto the wicker, pulling it from the gargoyle's side in the process. I layered the five elements in a destructive pentagram, embedded it in the quartz, and inverted it, all before the purifier reknit the weave down the length of the wicker. Coating the open wound of the drilled hole with gargoyle-tuned patches took a little longer, as I had to compensate for the variations within the marmot. It wasn't my best work, but it'd hold until the squad could destroy the purifier.

I shifted to the next quartz, only to be brought up short as the magic I'd been using pulled away from me, taking bits and pieces of me with it. I scrabbled with metaphysical fingers to regain control.

"Easy. Hang on," Seradon said, squeezing my fingers until the bones ground together.

My eyes snapped open. The polarized magic fluctuated and dimmed as one of the squad siphoned a chunk of elemental wood through the shield and released it harmlessly into the air. The pressure of the purifier slackened, but the maneuver had weakened the shield's structure, and the squad strained to hold it together, using every scrap of our combined magic.

"I'm going to pull you out for a second."

I gasped as my part of the link flew up the wicker of the purifier, scattering tatters of the self-replicating helixes, then shot into the shield. The pressure of the polarized elements burst through my senses. The separation Seradon had maintained slipped, jerking my awareness to the bombarded shield. Magic dragged from me as someone— Winnigan? Grant?—wove increasingly complex patches, manipulating the elements faster than I would have been able to follow if I hadn't been part of the link. I watched in awe as more than thirty strands around the shield shifted and knotted into discrete patterns—at once. And I'd been impressed with being able to invert a tiny pentagram!

Inside the shield, the elements swirled more volatile than before. The sections I'd capped pulsed with new intensity, vibrating against the shield with increased strength.

"Oh no," I whispered. In protecting the gargoyle, I'd forced the magic to switch directions, and it hammered the shield with heightened ferocity.

"What happens if it breaks the shield?" I asked.

"We don't want to find out. Hold on; we're going back in."

Hold on? To what? I tried to find myself in the vast collective of energy, but it was like trying to find particles of my breath once it mingled with the air. Seradon fortunately had no problem. She scooped me out of the connection and together we slid through the shield, then plowed down a loop of expensive woven phoenix feathers, battering through the purifier's weave of wood and air.

The gargoyle's insides were worse than before, not better. I'd removed the purifier's water and wood anchors, but now magic pulsed uneven bursts into and out of the air, fire, and earth anchors, destabilizing the gargoyle's body with increased speed. The feedback of pain was muted, as distant as the gargoyle's life itself. We were losing him.

I prepared to slice through the earth element, fusing the third quartz crystal to the marmot's neck, only to be abandoned in limbo when the squad pulled magic through me to reinforce the shield again.

"This is bad," Marciano said.

My body floated far away, and having magic drawn from me doubled the sensation. Seradon held us in place this time, but her grip felt tenuous, and if I lost my focus on the quartz, I was afraid I'd be blown apart and trapped in the purifier's mutant weave.

"Can you slow down, Mika?" Grant asked.

"No." Not without sacrificing the gargoyle. "I need to go faster. The gargoyle is being torn apart."

"Do you have to make the purifier stronger?" Velasquez asked, his deep voice strained.

"The blockades are the only way to stop it from feeding off the gargoyle," Seradon said. "She's doing the right thing."

"Then we'll hold it," the captain said.

I didn't want to voice my doubts. They were a full-five squad. They knew far better than me what they were capable of, but it seemed like they could barely maintain the shield on the purifier now. When I blocked the last three links, the strain on them would be enormous, but I wasn't going to waste time arguing.

I delved into the quartz. Power leapt to my bidding again, and in a few swift cuts, I'd disconnected the crude implant, reshaped the quartz, and created and inverted a destructive pentagram, blocking the purifier's third link with the gargoyle. Applying the finishing patches took less tweaking this time; I was getting good at predicting the marmot's imbalance.

The magic available to me through the link squeezed down to a trickle.

"Captain?" Velasquez asked.

I didn't wait for Grant to respond. I dove for the next quartz. The purifier pulsed fire into the gargoyle, and vats of magic shot out of the gargoyle through the only other remaining link. If I cut away one quartz connection, the other would continue to feed polarized magic into the gargoyle. Without an outlet, it would fill the helpless marmot and shred his insides.

"Spin the shield," the captain said, his voice distant. "Set it on a counterpattern."

The shield bounced into a riotous, distracting pattern. I scrambled to reorient on the quartz, the gargoyle, anything to define my individuality. I latched on to the marmot, sinking an elemental balance into him, then jumping to correct the levels of my magic to match the internal structure of the abused gargoyle.

"Give it a destructive layer," Grant said.

"I'm going to break the last two at once," I said, talking over the others. I didn't have the ability to maintain my individuality, divide magic across the gargoyle to the two separate quartz bolts, *and* keep up with their conversation. "I think . . . I think that will cause the purifier to break up."

"That'd be lucky," Velasquez said, his voice close.

I readied the destructive pentagrams, holding them next to the gargoyle where the elemental magic remained in its natural state. The pentagrams slowly grew when they should have remained static, and I realized with fresh horror that the gargoyle was passively feeding its magic to me, to all of us, despite the copious amounts being drained from him by the purifier. I'd been wrong. He wasn't doing anything to fight back or protect himself.

"Now." I pulled on the magic of the link. It responded like taffy, but I demanded more. "I need to do this now." I yanked, and for a second I felt Seradon, then the others beyond her. I think the captain said something, but whether it was encouragement or protest, I didn't hear.

I slammed the pentagrams in place at the same time as I cut the quartz from the gargoyle. With separate strands, I reshaped the quartz into flat barriers and simultaneously shoved wads of jasper-tuned patches into the wounds before pulling the pentagrams through the quartz and inverting them.

The barriers snapped into place, and the world exploded.

4

The concussion tossed me into the air, and I landed on my back, half on top of a boulder. My head snapped against something marginally softer than granite. Blackness swooped through my vision; then my collapsed lungs inflated, and I sucked in a harsh breath. I stared at the sky and listened to my ears ring, the world as fuzzy as the fluffy clouds high above me. Twists of earth and fire canopied above me in a protective dome of magic—one I wasn't holding.

Raw panic jolted through me, and I snatched at the elements, terrified the blast had burned through me and left me nullified, able to see the elements but never work them again. Fire and a smaller amount of air, earth, wood, and water trickled into me along misaligned pathways. I sagged with relief. It wasn't the full amount I could usually draw, but I would heal. I was still a heal—

Oliver!

I jackknifed up—or tried to. The ground shifted beneath my butt and a steel band pinned my torso. I twisted, trying to see what trapped me. Seradon lay beside me, though slightly lower. She blinked groggily at the sky, blood trickling from her nose. I squirmed to try to reach her.

"Easy now," Velasquez said, his deep voice startlingly close. More surprising, I'd felt the rumble of his words against my back. I was lying on top of the fire elemental! How had that happened?

The steel band lifted, and my brain finally put the obvious together: Velasquez had cushioned me and protected me from the blast. The boulder I thought I'd landed on had been his chest.

Above us, the protective shield dissipated. Velasquez helped me roll off him and I pushed to a sitting position, gasping when a fiery jab of pain shot through the top of my right shoulder. Tentatively, I investigated the pain with my fingers, sucking in air through clenched teeth when I encountered a splinter protruding from my skin. I craned my neck to see, setting off a fresh wave of pain.

"Hold still." The two words were the only warning Velasquez gave me before he yanked the splinter free. Groaning, I studied the twisted shard he held up for my inspection. It looked like a frozen ribbon of blood; then I recognized the thin carnelian shape of my earring. I touched my earlobe. The delicate strands had all broken into jagged pieces. I patted at my neck, feeling the wetness of several cuts but no more embedded pieces.

"Did you get cut?" I asked, turning to check Velasquez as I took the back off the earring and let it drop.

"Not from those." He brushed the front of his gray shirt, shedding sparkles of carnelian as he turned to help Seradon. She sat with her head in her hands, elbows on her knees, her posture an eerie echo of Elsa's when I'd first seen her.

"I'll live," she said, blotting blood from her upper lip with the hem of her shirt.

"Look at me," Velasquez said, touching my chin. He knelt in front of me, leaning close, and I hadn't seen him move. His blue eyes filled my vision. They weren't a flat color; rather, they had striations of darker agate and flecks of onyx. Lapis lazuli, I decided, arrested by their unexpected beauty.

The thought snapped my brain back to solid ground. Worry pinched Velasquez's full lips. With unexpectedly gentle fingers, he pulled the skin down beneath one of my eyes, then the other. Impatiently, I tracked his finger. When he shifted to examine my shoulder, I resumed my search for Oliver.

The blast had thrown us over ten feet beyond the pentagram, into the dirt. The others had been flung farther and were scattered around the pentagram plateau. No one appeared gravely injured, but everyone moved gingerly.

Elements hung heavy in the air, or more precisely, earth shimmered thick enough to give the illusion of being tangible. A wall of fire and earth hung on invisible strings to my right.

The blood drained from my head. It was more than a wall; it was the same barrier I'd seen inside the purifier's loops. Elongated and distorted and arching twice as tall as Grant, hundreds of helixes spun in an interlocking weave to create an impenetrable barrier between the two elements. The wall extended over thirty feet beyond the marmot before dipping down to touch the ground, but the complex braid of helixes that had previously been linked to the loop inside the purifier shot in a straight line toward the horizon. Four other evenly spaced elemental braids speared outward from the marmot like spokes on a wheel, and I didn't need to move to know the magic in between each would look equally dense and singular.

"You'll be fine," Velasquez said. "You're not as fragile as you look."

I wasn't paying attention. I'd spotted Oliver.

He lay in a crumpled heap below the pillar where he'd been perched. I lurched to my feet, catching myself with one hand on the ground when the world dipped and my legs buckled. Pushing back to my feet, I half crawled, half ran to the gargoyle, passing through the purifier's fire-earth and air-fire walls without resistance.

"Oliver!" I fell beside him and slapped a hand to his side, gathering magic to examine him. Air leapt to my call, but the other elements I needed to balance the magic felt as if they existed on the other side of a mountain of sand. "Oliver, come on. Wake up."

Bright red-orange eyes popped open, and Oliver lifted his head. His square jaw fell open in a dragon's smile. I sucked in a full breath, releasing it with a breathy sob of relief. Scooting back, I gave him room to right himself. Together we examined his wings and limbs, equally relieved to find him whole. I tried again to pull the blend of elements necessary to test Oliver's internal health, but once more only air responded.

"How do you feel?" I asked.

"Drained."

"It's no wonder," Seradon said, stopping beside me and wriggling her jaw to pop her ears. "I'd be toast without you. If you ever want to join a squad, you can be part of my team anytime, Oliver."

The half-grown dragon preened. I watched his movements closely, pleased not to see any stiffness or tenderness.

"His extra boost of magic right before the explosion gave me the strength I needed to cocoon us both," Seradon said to me. "The purifier—and we really need a better name for this monstrosity—seared through my shield and drilled into my head like it knew where to look. Without Oliver, we'd both be burned out."

I shuddered. "Thank you."

"Yep, that's what we do." Seradon gave me a gentle pat on the back before striding to Grant's side.

Burned out. My fingers trembled as I tightened my ponytail, and it took a moment for me to process the red sparkles tipping my fingers when I examined them. Carefully, I reached for my left earring. A few shards remained fused to the post and powdery pieces of orange-red quartz clung to my neck and scalp. I used my shirtsleeve to protect my fingers as I pulled the earring out; then I dropped it to the ground next to the pillar.

"Thank you, too, Oliver. You're amazing."

"Yep, that's what I do." Oliver grinned at his almost perfect imitation of Seradon's inflection. I smiled, feeling my world right itself. One gargoyle safe, one to go.

I rose with a modicum of grace this time, but my legs were wobbly and I braced against the pillar until I felt steady enough to walk. Flexing the fingers of my right hand hurt, and I examined the swelling around my middle finger's second knuckle. Blood oozed from a scrape, but it was coagulating. Considering I could have been nullified, a hurt knuckle seemed trivial.

Pushing away from the pillar, I headed for the marmot. Oliver yelped and stumbled into me, knocking me sideways. With a weird hopping kick, he jetted forward, then spun back toward me.

"What was that?" I rubbed my calf, where his alula had clipped me.

"That hurt!" Oliver pointed to the purifier braid separating the air and fire sections of the expanded bubble of polarized magic. I'd passed through the weave without feeling anything. I reached for the elements to test him, but now only fire responded. Frustrated, I had to rely on Oliver's assurance that the pain had been temporary.

"Okay. Stay here until we get this sorted."

Oliver nodded and curled his tail tight to his body. Hunched, he looked half his normal size, and I wished I'd insisted the young gargoyle wait outside the park, or better yet, at the library where he'd be safe.

I skirted a dirt-churned crater, realizing only when I saw sparkles of carnelian glinting in the indent that the divot was from the impact of Velasquez and me, or more accurately, the impact of Velasquez's body as he shielded me. I had more than Seradon and Oliver to thank for my relatively unharmed state.

From a distance, the marmot looked the same. He stood in the same position on his haunches, wings draped down his back and antlers arching skyward. Scraps of metal, wicker, alabaster, and glass littered the surrounding area and caught in the gargoyle's antlers. The horrific purifier had been reduced to nothing more than loose trash. A breeze lifted shredded phoenix feathers into the air, and I waved a hand in front of my face to keep them out of my eyes.

The elements swirled through an elongated vortex stretching from the marmot's toes up past his antlers. I tilted my head, trying to make sense of the chaotic magic through the dense swirl of fire element. When my brain made the belated connection, I sidestepped into the earth zone to double-check. My heart beat in my ears as I crouched to run a finger through a bright white radial line on the ground. A fine powder of quartz gritted against my fingertip. The explosion had pulverized my five quartz barriers, but perversely my inverted pentagrams had inflated to dwarf both me and the marmot. Worse, they appeared to be working as anchors for the purifier, holding it in place. Not only had I made the purifier explode, but I'd also made it stronger.

Just peachy.

I couldn't tell if the mutated pentagrams rested against the marmot or if the infinitesimal gap remained between the gargoyle and the purifier. At least magic no longer pulsed from the marmot.

I scrabbled for the elements to heal him, and this time earth tumbled into me but nothing else.

I'd worked all the elements right after the blast. Why couldn't I touch more than one at a time now?

Because I wasn't cocooned inside Velasquez's protective ward, I reasoned. He must have trapped the elements inside the shield when he'd created it, before magic polarized around us. That explained why fire had been the strongest element at the time. I'd thought I'd injured the metaphysical pathways in my brain, but standing in the earth section, I could draw on as much earth as normal without strain.

Frustrated, I shoved my hands through the vortex of magic and planted them on the marmot's chest, ignoring the swirling magic pricking my skin with a thousand sharp needles. Again, I felt nothing, but even live gargoyles could be as still as stone and equally as cold to the touch. I needed magic to get inside him. I needed to fix the damage the purifier had caused before it was too late.

Out of options, I held on to earth and refined it down to

the thinnest strand of quartz possible. The destructive cycle spinning around my wrist made me clumsy, jolting earth into the tortured gargoyle when I meant to feather it against him. A delicate echo of the marmot's essence pushed back against the foreign intrusion, and I withdrew as gently as possible. His life signs were faint enough to be alarming, but he lived.

I couldn't help him, not with magic like this. I glanced to the horizon. The polarization had to wear off soon. The balanced elements on the outside of this bubble would eat through the divided magic and degrade the purifier's pattern. Until that happened, I had no way to assess the marmot's injuries or right the internal damage the purifier had wrought on the helpless gargoyle.

Yet somehow, the bubble looked larger than it had before.

"He's alive?" Oliver called from where he huddled several feet away.

"Yes, but it's like he's asleep."

"That's because he's dormant," Grant said. The squad convened around us, everyone looking at the marmot.

"A lot of gargoyles do this," Seradon said. "It's like they check out for a while. They still give power, some more freely than gargoyles who are awake, but they don't interact with anyone. They become sort of like quiet statues."

"For how long?" I asked.

Seradon shrugged. "I don't know. You haven't encountered this before?"

I shook my head, feeling like a hypocrite. I should know more about gargoyles than anyone. I was the gargoyle healer, after all.

"This guy's been dormant for years. Probably a decade or two, maybe longer," Grant said.

"He hasn't moved that whole time?" I shared a glance with Oliver. The young gargoyle looked as confused as I felt. The squad seemed to believe the marmot's catatonic state was normal, but I couldn't think of a reason a gargoyle would opt to mimic a statue, passively feeding *everyone* magic in the vicinity. They were usually more picky than that. Plus, gargoyles needed to eat at least a few times a month. "Can he move, if he wants to?"

"I guess so. Being dormant is probably what saved him from being torn apart by the purifier," Seradon said. "Don't fret so much. This is all part of a gargoyle's life cycle."

I frowned and nodded. She sounded confident, but in my healer heart I knew she was wrong. Nothing about the marmot's lifeless state was normal, but it explained his pockmarked skin. I suspected his internal health would have looked poor even before Elsa's interference. It also explained how she'd been able to surgically attach the abominable purifier: The marmot had been helpless to stop her. That hadn't prevented him from feeling the pain of the implants, though.

"Are there more like this? Dormant?" My swollen knuckle protested, and I relaxed my fisted hands.

"A few," Seradon said.

Shame burned in my veins. I'd been concentrating on sick gargoyles who came to me or who contacted me through their chosen families. I hadn't paid any attention to the welfare of the public gargoyles or those who couldn't even speak for themselves. I needed to step up my efforts as a healer. I couldn't leave gargoyles helpless to be preyed upon by psychopaths like Elsa, who saw them as tools and not living creatures.

"This is bad," Winnigan said. She walked around the marmot, eyes on the horizon.

"I'm done messing around," Grant said. "Form up a link."

"The damn thing did its best to burn me out, sir. I'm mud and won't be much use for hours," Seradon said.

Mud? Fresh guilt welled up on a wave of gratitude, and I tried to think of a more adequate way to thank her for saving me from being nullified. "I'm sorry" tumbled out.

Seradon chuckled. "Aww, civilian guilt. That's cute."

Velasquez snorted, but his expression was blank when I looked at him.

"We don't have hours," Grant said.

"Good thing we have Mika. She can take my place."

Grant pinned me with his sharp brown eyes. "It's not ideal but I can make it work."

I wasn't half the earth elemental Seradon was, as the explosion I'd unleashed just proved. With a sinking stomach, I looked around the group. They assessed me with neutral expressions, telling me without words that no one was happy to be stuck with me. I felt acute relief when Grant spoke and everyone shifted their attention to him.

"The polarized magic isn't dissipating on its own. Since the blast, it's gained at least ten feet in every direction. We need to break the constructive pattern."

I hugged my stomach. It hadn't been a trick of my imagination. Even the spokes looked longer, stretching far beyond the dome of polarized magic and disappearing into the park. They didn't need the marmot to feed from any longer; the purifier was self-sustaining and prepared to assimilate the entire city.

"I don't get it," Marciano said. "The purifier should have torn itself apart once it didn't have the gargoyle to feed on."

"I think it might be my fault," I said, waving a hand at

the intact inverted pentagrams. Grant had to be regretting allowing Velasquez and Seradon to talk him into letting me save the gargoyle. If not for the flicker of life in the marmot, I'd be regretting it, too.

"Placing blame or feeling guilty won't get us anywhere," Grant said. "We need to—"

The polarized fire section rolled over a lit gas pit. Raw elemental magic roared from the flames, surging into the polarization field. Even from over fifty feet away, the backwash of heat tightened my skin. The influx of energy flared against the seam between fire and earth, built up, then surged through the looping pattern of the stretched helixes, feeding into earth. Earth spewed energy into water, water sloshed into wood, wood shot into air, and the entire polarized bubble bulged outward in a powerful push that covered another five feet in every direction.

"That's going to be a problem," Velasquez said.

I studied the park with fresh eyes. Elemental magic was always strongest around the physical source, and Focal Park had been designed as a place of natural enhancement. Its pentagon shape reflected the five elements, and each section represented a dominant element, all radiating from the center of the park in a natural constructive order. Elsa had aligned her purifier exactly along those lines, so each polarized segment ate through the matching element section of the park.

"That woman couldn't have made a bigger mess if she tried," the captain said, echoing my thoughts.

Air and earth passively fed their polarized sections, but in a few feet, the wood section would reach the entrance to the botanical gardens, and a dozen more gas torches and fire pits aligned with the fire field's path. If the polarization fields reacted to those as they had the small fire pit, this bubble of messed-up energy would expand in alarming leaps. Currently the only obstacles in the purifier's way were the smaller pieces of balancing elements in every section—a fountain in the fire section, a wind chime in the earth section—and us.

"If this reaches the river, it could swallow the city," Winnigan said, staring off into the distance where sunlight glinted off Lincoln River directly in the path of the polarized water section.

"Or it could negate it," Velasquez said. "That much water at once could overwhelm everything and cause the whole mess to collapse."

His words gave me hope, but if Winnigan was right and the city's elements divided into five separate sections, Terra Haven would fall apart. Everything from basic house-keeping magic to the complex structural patterns of the city's communication and transportation networks would collapse.

Not to mention the devastation to lives. We were proof that humans could function in the polarized fields, even if magic wasn't working right, but some creatures depended on the blended elements for sustenance. Stuck in this divided energy, gargoyles throughout the city would sicken from the imbalance and be forced to flee the city or die.

"We're not letting it reach the river," Grant said. "We're countering this now. Spread out to your element and link."

The squad traded glances and hustled to their sections. Seradon strode to my side and gave me quiet directions.

"This is different than what we did before, and it's going to hurt. Since you can't access all the elements, the link will have to act as one person. Grab earth and push it to Winnigan, then let Velasquez push fire to you."

Earth element burrowed into me, sharp as shale without another element to buffer it, but no matter how much I drew or how hard I pushed, I couldn't penetrate the barrier between earth and water. The magic I fed into the wall of helixes warped and transformed into water, exiting the barrier in a useless splash. Around the circle, the captain, Marciano, Winnigan, and Velasquez were each haloed in an impressive display of elemental magic, but everyone had the same problem I did. Worse, our efforts fed the purifier, and the bubble pushed outward.

Grant cussed. "Stand on the dividing lines and try again."

We all shifted to the right. Sweat trickled down my neck, stinging my cuts. Keeping my eyes on the marmot, I aligned myself in the middle of the purifier's wall, with polarized fire encasing the right side of my body and earth the left side. The helixes moved harmlessly through me—until I tried to grab an element. I reached for earth first, and magic pounded out of control against my brain. Refining my draw down to a slender strand enabled me to manipulate the element, but the moment I opened myself to more, earth crashed through me, breaking my hold and leaving my metaphysical pathways bruised. Reversing tactics, I reached for fire. It roared into me, overwhelming and unchecked, then guttering to a mere flutter too soft to grasp. Heat beat against my right side and charred my elemental senses. Through sheer determination, I clung to a whipcord of fire and yanked it to me.

Between one second and the next, the fire element morphed into earth inside me. With a cry, I threw the wild energy from me before it ripped me apart. I staggered into Seradon, gasping for air. Pain speared through my skull, subsiding to a dull headache as I clutched my temples.

Elements didn't do that. It would have been like having a real flame in a fireplace turn spontaneously into molten lava. The elements could feed and support each other, but they didn't transform.

"You okay?" Seradon asked.

I straightened and nodded. To the right, Velasquez collapsed to one knee, a beam of raw fire shooting from his palm into the sky. Shaking his head, he surged to his feet. Marciano knocked himself flat on his back, and grass sprang up around the left side of his body, covering him in seconds. Around the circle, the polarized bubble surged and churned, eating across more parkland.

"Stop!" Grant ordered. "This is useless. We need to be on the outside where we can get some damn control."

The squad convened in the earth section. Sweat matted Velasquez's shirt to his chest and ran down his neck. He stuck an arm back into the hot air of the fire section, then retracted it.

"That's not natural," he muttered.

"We can't predict how this'll mutate, but we should be safest in our element," the captain said. "Divide up and get to the outside. We'll link up once we're clear."

"I prefer not to cook," Velasquez said. "I'll go with Mika."

"Good. She'll need your help. Seradon, you're with Winnigan until you're clear, then get to a healer and get back here ASAP."

"Aye, sir."

I fervently hoped Seradon's recovery could be sped up by a healer. With any luck, she'd be back to assist with the link, because I was far out of my league. So far all I'd managed to do was buy the marmot gargoyle a little time, and in the process I'd unleashed a diabolical energy intent on unraveling the very structure of magic. I hadn't exactly proven myself to be a competent stand-in.

Oliver paced the purifier's braid between earth and fire, working himself up to jump through. He'd been hanging back out of the way since he couldn't assist us. I wished I could do the same.

"Captain, I'd like Oliver to go with you," I said, motioning the young gargoyle to stay put. I was tempted to keep Oliver at my side for our mutual comfort in this bizarre situation, but I had to think of his safety. With access to only one element, we were all vulnerable to unknown dangers. Oliver would be a lot safer under Grant's protection than mine. A person didn't become captain of an FPD squad without learning how to defend himself with and without magic. If things got dangerous, Grant would be able to take care of the adolescent gargoyle.

Grant gave me an assessing look, and his nod said he approved. "Oliver, you're with me. Clear out."

"Mika?" Oliver asked, and the confusion in his tone made my heart hurt.

"It's okay. You'll be safe with Captain Monaghan."

"What about you?"

"Are you really doubting this guy?" I hooked a thumb in the direction of Velasquez's broad chest. "We'll meet up on the outside. Hurry but stay safe."

The squad split into their elements and moved out at a jog. Oliver darted through the braid between the air and fire section and shook off the pain, then broke into a lope, easily keeping up with the captain.

As much as I wanted to watch them until they disappeared, I forced myself to turn back to the marmot. Planting a hand on his cool stomach, I said, "Hang in there. I'll be back for you."

Shaking the tingling pain of the inverted pentagram from my hand, I pivoted to face the expanding front line of the earth section. "Let's get out there and break this thing once and for all." My attempt at bravery made my words come out harsher than I intended.

With a faint smile curving his lips, Velasquez saluted me.

5

Once we cleared the sycamore trees around the central pentagon, the ground flattened into bisecting stone pathways and gravel mazes shaded by cottonwoods. The paths to the right led to the arched bridges and meandering trails of the water section, where willow trees lined the banks of intertwining streams. To the left, the shallow slope of the fire section Kylie and I had run down shimmered with unnatural heat.

Velasquez steered us up the middle toward the shallow-tiered rock gardens, and we jogged up the steps, me huffing, Velasquez silent. The polarized bubble had advanced over a hundred yards from the center of the park, and at the rate we were moving, we'd clear it in a few minutes. Earth weighted my skin, shard-sharp and oppressive. I drew on it just to touch it. Even unlinked and unaided by a gargoyle, I held double the amount I normally could. The element was so pure it could pull the dust particles from the very air. I could reshape the ground with it as easy—

I jumped when Velasquez touched my arm.

"Hold up. It's reached the reflection pool. I want to see what happens."

Velasquez pointed to the fire section, but I scanned the air section beyond it, looking for Oliver. I found Grant first. He ran against a crosswind, and sand lifted and eddied around his ankles, partially obscuring Oliver loping at his side.

In the fire section, the leading edge of the polarized magic touched the edge of a shallow pool of water almost twenty feet across, and the magic stuttered around us. Water element rising from the physical liquid clashed with fire, extinguishing a patch of polarized element. The influx of fire magic feeding into the earth section slowed, and the advancing border of the entire polarization bubble halted. The weight of earth against my senses eased.

I spun. On the opposite side of the earth section, water still drank down the earth element through the earth–water seam. Magic continued to push through the constructive weave—water into wood, wood into air—draining the magic from each section. Before I could celebrate, the built-up energy hit the air–fire border and whooshed through, strengthening the fire element. The calm waters of the reflection pool burst into a boil. Steam gushed into the air as the entire pool evaporated. Fresh fire magic fed into the earth section, constricting earth around my skin again, and the outer rim of the bubble jumped several yards, negating the progress we'd made to the border.

"So much for that," Velasquez said, turning back toward our goal and setting a ground-eating pace.

I fell in behind him, gasping when I caught sight of his back. Long rips in the shirt of his gray uniform exposed bleeding cuts and pebble-embedded abrasions.

"Good thing I came with you," he said. "Otherwise it

would have been Marcus flambé." When I didn't respond, he shot me a look over his shoulder. "What, too graphic?"

"Your back. I thought your uniform had protection weaves in it."

"It did. That blast, this"—he gestured to the polarized energy around us—"burned through it."

My hand lifted to my own torn sleeve, the only damage my unspelled clothing had taken during the explosion. My skin beneath it was unharmed. "Ah, did I thank you for . . ." Would it be too dramatic to say *saving my life*?

"Letting you use me like an air cushion?" Velasquez grinned.

I caught my breath. The man needed a permit for a smile like that. Maybe that's why he didn't pull it out much. He should, though.

"I couldn't invite you to the party, then let you get hurt," he said.

"You have a weird idea of a party." I stepped around a bench seat and into a well of pain.

Invisible bonds wrapped around my legs to my waist, and agony welled from my bones, burrowing outward through my joints and my skin. I screamed and wrenched to free myself. Nothing held me, yet I couldn't move. I folded forward to clutch my legs—

"No! Don't!"

—and the trap slid over my head. Pain pulled from my pores, and I flailed against the invisible bonds, gasping on air too thick to breathe. My foot shifted. I clawed for magic, but even earth didn't respond. A hollow nothingness pressed back where magic should have existed, stunning me. I could see the element eddying above my head, but I couldn't reach it and none penetrated the invisible spherical barrier holding me.

Velasquez thrust his arm into the air beside me, fingers splayed. Thick bands of earth pushed from his fingertips, the movement of the element the most beautiful magic I'd ever seen. The trap eroded and distorted the magic, flattening it and almost extinguishing it before feathery tendrils brushed the inside edge of the invisible sphere. It imploded, and magic sucked into the void, the raw earth sharp and welcoming.

I collapsed sideways, rubbing the fading cramps from my legs as the pain ebbed from my body.

"What *was* that?" I asked, accepting Velasquez's help up.

"A null pocket. When the purifier exploded, this nook of balanced elements must have canceled each other out."

I glanced around. The five elements were equally represented in a tight circle around the stone bench. Dozens such setting existed throughout Focal Park. "Why didn't it get consumed by the earth?"

Velasquez shrugged. "We're dealing with bizarre magic. Somehow that tiny explosion took down the ward, too, which doesn't make any sense."

I was so used to seeing the park without the ward, I hadn't noticed it was missing.

"We don't know what we're dealing with, so watch where you step." He resumed his march toward the front edge of the polarization field.

"Sure. I'll keep my eye out for invisible pockets of nothing," I muttered as I trotted to catch up with his long-legged stride. I fell into step beside him. "Why did it hurt?" I asked, speaking loud enough for him to hear this time. I'd been cuffed with null bands before, and they'd slid a barrier between me and the elements, but they hadn't inflicted pain.

"It was pulling the magic from you."

"But why? Why couldn't I walk through it?"

"Nulls are balanced voids. When you bungled into it, it reacted as if you were the enemy. It couldn't let you keep walking. It had to destroy the magic inside you, so it trapped you."

"You make it sound like it had the ability to think."

"A poor analogy, then. It reacted to the magic in you the same way fire reacts to paper: You were consumable."

What a pleasant thought.

"Usually null pockets deteriorate on their own, and pretty fast, but I don't trust the elements to act normally right now."

As if to reinforce his words, the earth moved beneath our feet like a blanket being shaken out. A low rumble rolled up the hill, drowning out the creaking protests of the cottonwoods. I flung out my arms for balance, managing to keep my feet beneath me. Velasquez widened his stance and rode the undulating ground like he'd done it a dozen times before. My legs continued to tremble even after the granite resumed its characteristic inert state.

"Stay close and stay behind me."

Velasquez's matter-of-fact tone snapped me into motion. Following in his footsteps, I jogged across sun-warmed rocks, my feet slapping the hard stone in tandem with his. We had at least another twenty feet to go before we reached the edge of the polarization field, all of it uphill, and I couldn't shake the feeling that we were moving too slowly. It was all well and good to be safe and conserve our energy instead of making a headlong dash, but the longer we were inside the polarized magic, the more my skin crawled with the need to escape.

The granite shivered beneath my feet, the smooth wind-worn rock growing rough and uneven between one step and the next. I glanced around. None of the other rocks in our section were moving or reshaping. The earth was responding to our footsteps.

"Velasquez . . ."

"I see it." The fire elemental altered his stride, his footsteps landing softer without him slowing. I tried to do the same and fell behind.

Velasquez jumped to a wide boulder a step above us. I'd barely cleared the step behind him when the boulder sprouted a short wall in front of Velasquez, solid rock reshaping as fast as a blink. With speed I'd never have accredited to the large man, he sprang to the right. A crest of speckled gray granite swirled behind his feet, the dense rock moving and re-forming like water but sounding like a landslide. When he landed, a sheet of schist shot skyward at his right side, dwarfing him. Velasquez slammed into it, the impact bouncing him back a half step. Schist bulged from the wall and frothed up the smooth surface, coating it in short, jagged peaks.

I slammed a knee into the protrusion Velasquez had avoided and windmilled my arms to counter my forward momentum. The granite beneath me lifted, carrying me toward Velasquez. He grabbed my arm, balancing me as the rocks ground to a halt.

Neither of us moved, our ragged breathing filling the space between us. Velasquez was a foot shorter than me, standing in a knee-deep hole and hemmed in on two sides by rock walls where moments before there'd been a flat expanse of granite. I swallowed hard.

The earth growled behind me, and I twisted to look. A ridge of brown-and-black-banded hornfels pushed upward along the dividing line between the earth and fire section in an inches-high mountain range, with a few peaks sprouting as high as my thighs. Up and down the helix wall, the earth rumbled in an ever-growing and shifting barrier.

"What the—" A heavy crack louder than ten gargoyles landing on marble drowned out Velasquez's curse. We both spun toward the sound. A waist-high block of granite large enough for me to stand on punched from the dirt at the leading edge of the bubble. In rapid succession, three more burst from the soil like jagged teeth in the mouth of the polarized bubble.

"The air," I said, swallowing twice before I coaxed sound from my throat. "It's damming it. Or trying to." In the destructive cycle, earth stopped air. Based on the twisted logic of this polarized magic, it made sense that the raw earth wouldn't tolerate the movement of air. When Velasquez had jumped, he'd created a breeze, and the granite had grown to halt it. When he'd jumped the second time to avoid the sudden growth, he'd created even more air displacement, and the rock had boxed him in to cut it off.

"Look." I crouched. It hurt the cut on my shoulder to maintain my grip on Velasquez's arm and bend down, but I couldn't make myself let go. Leaning forward, I huffed out a sharp breath. Schist bubbled out of a vein in the granite and formed a shallow bowl around the puff of air, effectively stopping the wind.

"Crap," Velasquez said.

"Yep."

"Okay. I'm going to get out of this hole before it closes in on me."

I straightened and braced myself. Velasquez planted one foot on the granite next to me, then eased himself free of the earthen trap. A sharp spiral of granite shot upward from the base of the hole, counteracting the downdraft of air

Velasquez displaced. I yanked him toward me before the sharp tip could puncture his back.

Velasquez stumbled against me, catching me in his arms before I could move my feet.

"Maybe we should move to the water section," I said, my nose pressed against his broad chest. He smelled of sweat and dirt, and it wasn't a bad combination.

"I don't think it would help."

We eased apart without moving our feet and I leaned to look around him at the water section. The ground had risen to create a crenelated wall along the water–earth boundary, damming overflowing streams that had previously lazed throughout the earth section. Deeper in the water section, a pond burbled, then fountained, fed from an underground geyser. It overflowed its banks and flooded the breadth of the water section. Seconds later, the magic influx cycled around the purifier's constructive bubble and hit earth.

Velasquez and I staggered as the density of our air thickened with unnatural gravity. At the edge of the central pentagon, a sycamore tree toppled, and the ground rose up to break its fall. Cascading ridges of earth halted the rush of air up the tiers, curling back over the fallen tree and toppling a few cottonwoods, restarting the process. I pressed one ear to Velasquez's chest, clapping a hand over the other to muffle the cacophony. Beneath us, the ground quaked and I rode it out on trembling knees.

Thick black smoke billowed into the sky where the top of the sycamore had fallen into the fire section. In rapid succession, three more smoke columns joined the first and heat tightened the air even as more power flooded into the earth section and the leading edge of the polarization jumped several yards.

I lifted my head from Velasquez's chest to watch

Winnigan and Seradon wade into the growing pond, then dive beneath the surface. Both women emerged a few feet away, arms paddling as they swam. A current pulled them away from us toward the wood section, where the pond cascaded down a waterfall that hadn't existed ten minutes ago.

"What's happening to the ground in the wood section?" I asked. The earth eroded under the falling water as if it were sand, not hardy granite, hornfels, and schist.

"The same thing that's happening here. Wood destroys earth."

With growing horror, I examined the wood section. The ground around the central pentagram was pockmarked with holes like empty graves. Farther away, the ground disappeared as if sheared off at the front edge of overgrown creosote bushes, and the gnarled roots of the botanical garden's red maples twisted in the open air. The trees' trunks were twice as thick as they'd started the day, and I realized the movement of the visible roots wasn't caused by the wind; I was seeing the trees grow.

Through the trunks, I caught a glimpse of two figures. Marciano and Grant slogged through the boggy ground. Marciano carried a branch he used to prod the ground before advancing, like a man moving across snow, looking for hidden crevasses.

Oliver wasn't with the captain.

I whipped my head the other direction, blindly grabbing Velasquez's forearms to steady myself as I squinted to see the air section through the bordering fire section. Heat waves bent the light and made the horizon dance. I couldn't make out any of the park's tall sculptures or windmills, and my knuckles tightened on Velasquez's sleeves.

My breath whooshed out when I finally spotted Oliver.

He flew above what looked like a smear of khaki. Sand. The heat of fire wasn't distorting the view; the growing winds had kicked up a sandstorm.

Oliver flapped his wings, then retracted them, plummeting into the sand before flapping slowly aloft again. His long body jerked against the wind before he dropped out of sight again.

"What's he doing?"

"Conserving energy," Velasquez said.

Oliver emerged from the sand again, long wings beating almost too slow. As he rose, the air barrier near him flared and blew magic into fire.

"He's trying not to stir up air," I said. *Damn it, I should have brought him with me.*

Oliver couldn't land, because he'd be blind. He hadn't been able to go with the captain because he would have been swallowed by the eroding soil. If the wood section was anything like the earth, he wouldn't have been able to fly through it. Gargoyles were made of stone; they required air magic to stay aloft, and the wood section with its polarized magic wouldn't have had any air for Oliver to use.

"We need to get moving. Slowly," Velasquez said.

A thunderous crack of rock lifting against a breeze coming from outside the polarization field echoed the urgency in his tone. Velasquez turned and took a cautious step. Small peaks of granite lifted on either side of his foot from the push of air, but the bulk of the boulder beneath us remained still.

"Follow close," he said.

Every rumble and clatter of moving earth grated against my nerves. In between the unnatural earthen shifts, the only sound audible was our footsteps. The lap of water against the growing dam on the right, the waterfall cascading into the wood section, the windstorm Oliver battled—all the destruction reshaping the park should have raised a racket.

"I think the air is getting denser," I said. It was harder to draw a breath, and it wasn't because we were walking up an increasingly steep incline.

"All the more reason to hurry," Velasquez agreed as he took another careful, agonizingly slow step. I tried to laugh, but it came out as a breathy whimper.

We hiked up the middle of the earth section more than thirty feet from the fire section, but heat radiated against my left side and sweat rolled down my spine. I focused on Velasquez's feet, doing my best to step exactly where he did. Every ripple he caused doubled with my passing, building a ragged sluice into the boulders. After a handful of steps, narrow blades popped up between my feet when one foot passed the other. High-pitched but soft squeaks accompanied each sharp formation.

A few steps later, the earth crumpled and sharpened beneath my boots in response to the puffs of air stirred by Velasquez's feet. Moving gingerly, I tiptoed after him, every step becoming increasingly sharp and uneven. I'd stopped checking our progress against the leading edge of the earth section. It was too depressing. Everything that slowed us down only increased the strength of the purifier, and the bubble pushed outward at a steady, ground-eating pace. Despite the distance we'd covered, we were still a dozen yards from escaping.

Lightning split the sky beside us in the fire section, sounding like it exploded against my eardrums. I jumped. The granite beneath me reacted, spearing straight into my foot.

I screamed on an inhale, the sound sucking into my throat.

6

"What? Are you okay?"

Unable to speak, I pointed to my left foot. Velasquez twisted without shifting his feet, then cussed.

"Did it go through your foot?"

The sharp pain radiating from my sole scrambled my thoughts, and I fought the urge to yank my foot free. Any sudden movements could cause the granite to reshape around or *inside* my foot.

"I don't think so," I gasped. "Into but not through." Pain climbed up my leg until it felt like everything from my knee down had been pierced. I pictured the bottom of my foot and the rock penetrating it, and white noise rang in my ears, clouding my vision. A sharp snap next to my nose brought me back to myself.

"Hey. Stay with me. You need to lift your foot. Slowly. Then you're going to climb on my back and I'm going to carry you, okay?"

"No."

"No? What's your plan?"

"Your back. I can't—"

"My back is fine. Two steps will cause fewer rock ripples than four."

I shook my head. Arguing helped distract me from the compulsion to rip my foot free. "You're bleeding."

"So are you. If you're not afraid of getting a little of my blood on you, I'm not afraid of getting a little of your blood on me."

I shifted, biting my lip when pain shot up my leg.

"Okay," I said.

Velasquez offered me his arm and I clung to him while I inched my foot from the rock spike. Sweat coated my body when I was finally free. I crossed my foot over my knee and peeked at the bottom. The thin leather sole of my boot had been sheared through, and blood seeped from the arch of my foot. For a closer inspection, I'd have to remove my shoe, and I wasn't eager to see the wound or to jostle my foot that much.

"You're not walking anywhere on that," Velasquez said.

I nodded, not trusting my voice. The pain had morphed into a pulsing throb, and the thought of putting weight on my foot made me want to whimper.

"Grab my neck," Velasquez said, turning his back to me.

I stared at the dirt- and rock-crusted scrapes in his back. I wouldn't be able to hold on without hurting him.

"Maybe you should go on without me. If I don't move, I should be okay until you guys shut this down."

"You're being dramatic. Hop on and let's get going."

I grasped his shoulders and lifted my left leg toward his hip but hesitated, unsure how to proceed.

"We'll be here all day if you try to do this without touching me."

"I don't want to hurt you."

With a growl, he crouched, grabbed my left thigh, and lifted me, stepping forward at the same time. I squeaked and slung my arms around his neck, pulling my right leg up to squeeze his hips. A solid curl of granite unfurled behind me, slapping my butt and jostling me against Velasquez. He grunted, then took a second cautious step.

"You okay?" he asked after three more steps. The granite shifted and bubbled behind us, folding on itself like a crumpled rug as it halted every current of air Velasquez's footsteps lifted.

"I think so."

Dirt sifted from Velasquez's thick hair when my head brushed it, and the loamy odor was comforting. Clinging to the fire elemental was akin to hugging a warm boulder, and I welcomed the illusion of safety that being pressed up against his strong body gave me.

"Good. Because I know we're trying not to move the air, but I need to breathe."

I felt him swallow against my forearm and hastily relaxed my stranglehold. Belatedly remembering his back, I did my best to shift my weight to the vise grip of my thighs around his hips while concaving my stomach away from his wounds.

"What are you doing?" Velasquez asked.

"Trying not to hurt you."

"Cut it out. You're making it worse." His footsteps hadn't slowed or altered during my adjustments.

"Sorry, Velasquez."

"Call me Marcus. And relax. I'm about as fragile as the gargoyles you heal."

"Modest, too, Marcus," I muttered, knowing he'd hear me.

He flexed, and his shoulder muscles hardened like

stones beneath my arms in a silent testament to his boast. I reminded myself that he had to be made of tough stuff to be in an FPD squad. A lot tougher than me. More tears than I was proud of had escaped while I'd been extricating my foot. I hoped he was too preoccupied to notice when they dripped from my chin to soak into his shirt.

"Hold tight. I'll have to take these stairs faster," Marcus said. His voice rumbled against my chest, and I realized I'd sagged against him. He'd made good time across the boulder field and had already reached the first unnatural block of granite. The front line of the polarization field expanded half as fast as a normal walking pace, with alarmingly frequent jumps as various parts of the massive constructive weave encountered fresh elemental magic to feed on. The crack and snap of growing rock had become a constant, and what had started as a handful of jutting teeth-like pillars along the front edge of the field had expanded to a series of uneven steps building toward the sky. The leading edge was already taller than Marcus. Only the rise of the hill naturally dampening the wind currents had prevented the pillars from shooting up higher.

I tightened my grip on Marcus as he powered up the first steep steps. Granite scraped and grated behind us, sounding as if the rocks were chasing us, a great attacking stone monster perpetually one step away from hamstringing Marcus and taking us both down for the kill.

Marcus let go of my right leg to use his hand for balance. I did my best to remain still on his back, both because it was the only way I could be helpful and because every time my foot was jarred, pain spiked all the way to my knee.

For several steps, Marcus moved parallel with the outer edge of the bubble and I could see the air section. I looked for Oliver, but I couldn't find him through the haze of the fire section. Lightning skittered through the polarized fire with increased frequency, held at bay by the flimsy-looking wall of the purifier's helixes. The bright flashes left afterimages on my vision; the thunder deafened me.

"Almost there," Marcus said through ragged breaths.

The leading edge of the polarization bubble stretched a few feet in front of us. Outside it, the interlocking helixes narrowed to a mass no thicker than my waist, and from our new height, I spotted the end of the fire–earth braid.

"Look! The purifier stops there." I pointed to a pile of boulders ahead of us and to our left. The fire–earth braid fed into the rocks, but it didn't come out the other side. "Maybe it's weakening." Given the oppressive stillness of the air and the swelling cacophony of the granite around us, I amended my hope. "Or it has a finite reach."

Marcus hopped to a higher pillar, sidestepping the curl of granite that followed his foot.

"Or it found another patient for you," he said.

I spotted the gargoyle among the boulders. The foxlike gargoyle's dull tigereye body and dirt-brown wings blended into the rocks—or they would have if a massive malicious braid of magic hadn't speared into her.

"Oh no! Hurry!" If she'd been subject to the purifier's dividing magic this whole time, it had to be tearing her apart.

"Working on it," Marcus grunted.

The ground beneath us rumbled and the pillars close to the edge of the field shifted and rose. Marcus cursed and danced across the top of the rocks, fighting for footing on the shifting tops. We were close to escape, but the leading edge of the bubble crept forward, pulling taller pillars into our path.

"I'm going to have to jump," Marcus shouted over the near-constant booming.

"Okay." If he could angle toward the hillside, the drop would be only a few feet, but first he had to clear the ever-rising cliff steps.

Marcus grabbed both my legs in a crushing grip. I tightened my arms around his shoulders.

"Here we go."

He sprinted up the shifting rocks, and I jounced on his back, eyes locked on the perpetually advancing edge of the field. Just as Marcus planted his foot on the last rising pillar and pushed off, the bubble shifted and grew by several feet at once. Granite burst from the inert ground beneath us, shooting toward our plummeting bodies.

I yanked earth magic to me and sheared off the top of the growing pillar before it could break Marcus's legs. His right foot clipped the edge of the pillar, but his left hit the top solidly. Working blindly on the rock beneath his feet, I drove pure earthen strands into the granite and stretched it the same way I would manipulate quartz. The grainy rock reshaped, as malleable as dough. Lifting the rock beneath Marcus's foot, I launched us toward safety.

We catapulted through the barrier, and my connection to the raw earth magic snapped. Blinded by the backlash, I lost my grip on Marcus and braced for impact with the rocky ground. It never came. Soft strands of air cushioned my fall. I opened my eyes, closing them just as quickly as the light refracted into a thousand razors inside my head.

I sucked in a breath, then another, savoring the light texture of the air in my lungs despite by body's conflicting pains.

"Am I dead?" I croaked.

"Mind blasted."

Clutching my head, I squinted in the direction of Marcus's voice. When the sunlight didn't slice my brain this time, I opened my eyes wider.

I sat on a large boulder a few feet up the hill from Marcus, and once he saw I could support myself, his bands of air and wood magic holding me up dissipated.

"Good move with the rock wave."

In a sea of pillars, one column of granite looked like it had melted toward us before being sheared off by a colossal blade. With the backlash of magic reverberating in my brain, it took me a moment to process the sight. I'd reshaped a couple hundred pounds of pure granite as easily as I might have a grape-size quartz seed crystal. That kind of strength couldn't be matched even by a full-spectrum earth elemental. Yet inside the polarized earth section, it'd been easy.

Mind blasted? Not fried, right? I scrambled for the elements, going limp when they responded. Reverently, I spun the five harmonious elements together, forming a basic pentagram and floating it in the air in front of me just to admire the beauty of the combined elements. The amount of earth I could hold was paltry compared to what I'd wielded inside the bubble, but I didn't care. Buffered and mixed with the other elements, earth felt smooth again, not sharp and raw like it had in the polarization field. It felt whole, and so did I. Out here, with all the elements working together, we had a chance at stopping Elsa's monstrosity.

First things first, we had to save the fox gargoyle.

I pushed to my feet—and fell back to the ground with a strangled gasp. The wound in my foot caused nauseous waves of pain to pulse through me, and I took shallow breaths until the urge to vomit subsided.

"Have you ever had a field patch?" Marcus asked.

I shook my head, keeping my lips pressed together.

"Oh, goodie. A virgin."

I jerked to look at his expression. He winked at me with an exaggerated leer obviously designed to distract me. I would have rolled my eyes, but he chose that moment to unlace my shoe. My fingers clawed into the soil, but I managed to contain most of my whimper as the shoe peeled from my foot. A fine slice of fire cut away my sock and it dropped to the rock.

"Hey, you'll live," Marcus said with irritating cheer. Something cold settled against my skin, then crept *into* the wound. It should have hurt or grossed me out, but the pain abated until only a cold spot remained, and I decided I'd never felt anything sweeter.

"What was that?"

"A field patch. A little water cooled to ice to block the nerves, a little earth to dam the bleeding, a little fire to counter infection. You'll need a healer and proper healing when we're done, but this will tide you over."

"It doesn't hurt," I said, awed. I shifted to pull my foot up to take a look, but Marcus captured my ankle.

"No. If you see it, you'll think about it too much. Let me wrap it."

Marcus knelt and spun tiny bands of fire around his midsection, slicing strips from the bottom of his shirt. With his pants riding low on his hips, the shortened shirt revealed a tanned stomach and a sculpted V of muscle veering into his waistband. I looked away. Having spent the last ten minutes clinging to his back, I knew Marcus didn't possess an ounce of fat—I didn't need to ogle the man for proof. Even if the view was a good deal more pleasant than anything else in my sight.

"If you teach me how to repeat the patch, I could put it on your back," I said.

"Just get some of the rocks out, and we'll call it even."

I waited for Marcus to say he was joking, but he didn't look up from my foot. He wound the strips of his shirt into a makeshift bandage, his speed silently reminding me that we didn't have any time to waste.

"Turn so I can see what I'm doing," I said.

I grimaced at the raw texture of Marcus's back. Carrying me had reopened the wounds, and they looked far worse than I remembered. My civilian guilt, as Seradon had called it, welled up stronger than ever. I glanced at the blood drying on my shirt, all his, and then got to work.

Wrapping a band of earth with soft layers of water, I dabbed the elements across his back. The water loosened the grit caked in the wounds and the earth pulled on all like matter. Bloody pebbles rolled down his back to the ground.

If he'd been as similar to a gargoyle as he'd boasted, I would have slid magic into him and healed him from the inside. Unfortunately, my earth elemental skills were useless on human physiology, and if I tried to push magic into him, I'd likely do more damage than good. My clumsy efforts were the best option, but it must have felt like I was picking at the cuts with my finger. I winced with the extraction of each tiny rock, but Marcus didn't react.

"I think that's the worst of it," I said as Marcus tied off the wrap on my foot.

"Good. We need to get moving. Here's your shoe."

The leather fit snug around the bandage, making me grateful I couldn't feel the puncture. When I stood, I put my full weight on my foot and all I felt was the cool press of Marcus's magic.

I looked for Oliver, and the view took my breath away.

Beyond the misshapen wedge of the earth section we'd escaped, an expanding triangle of the park lay scorched and strewn with embers. Flames belched from pockets in the ground and lightning crackled brilliant streaks through the shimmering hot air. Viewed through this, the air section beyond looked to be one giant sandstorm, and dirt hazed the sky above it. Oliver's slender orange-red body had been swallowed by the storm, and I fought the urge to run to find him. I should never have sent him with Captain Monaghan. Oliver was my responsibility, and now he was all alone and fighting through a sandstorm created by powerful, unpredictable magic.

Logically, I knew his humping lope would have been a disaster in the air-sensitive earth section. Oliver wouldn't have been able to fly to even out his gait, and while Marcus was strong, I doubted he could have carried me *and* Oliver out. It wouldn't do any good for me to get trapped in the sandstorm with Oliver, either, as much as I yearned to go help him.

Telling myself I wasn't abandoning Oliver, I hobbled a few steps toward the fox gargoyle. When the numbness in my foot held, I hurried to the base of the pile of boulders.

From this angle, the gargoyle was hidden. While I hunted for a foothold, I kept an eye on the leading edge of the creeping polarization bubble. At best, we had ten minutes to free the gargoyle before the field reached us.

"Here." Marcus indicated an almost natural staircase up the rocks on the other side of the boulders. I clambered up, trying not to rely on my injured foot. Just because I couldn't feel the wound didn't mean I wouldn't make it worse by stressing it.

I forgot about my foot when I reached the gargoyle. Hardly larger than a bear cub, she lay curled in a tight ball in the narrow bed of rocks, her long tigereye fox muzzle partially hidden under her thick tail. Up close, I could see her wings weren't dusty brown; they were a smoky citrine so gritty and scarred and covered with dirt that they looked brown. Her eyes were dim, as if she'd been sleeping when the purifier exploded and locked on to her. Or knocked unconscious. Her magic passively fed into and boosted the atrocious polarizing magic just as the marmot gargoyle's had. No quartz had been necessary to forge a connection between the purifier's braid and the fox, either; it'd burrowed in using raw power.

"I think if I can remove the braid, it'll be like unhooking an anchor," I said. "It might cause the purifier to unravel. Having another gargoyle to feed off of must be strengthening it."

"Okay. I'll check on the others."

Almost on top of his words, an air message opened above us and Winnigan's voice emerged. "We're out. Seradon's going to get healed. I'm headed your way."

Marcus responded as he continued to climb up the boulders toward the peak. Movement in the periphery of my vision pulled my head up. Seradon and Winnigan jogged across the flat sunbathing grounds, skirting the expanding polarization field. When she reached a natural path, Seradon peeled away, angling toward the tunnel exit. Despite having been magically stunted from the initial blast and then swimming her way out of the water section, she managed a cheerful wave and smile before she disappeared out of sight. In her place, I would have been dragging myself on all fours toward the nearest escape route. For all our sakes, I hoped a healer waited just outside the park, ready to repair Seradon's metaphysical pathways so she could rush back before the captain was ready to link.

Maybe the link wouldn't be necessary if I could break the purifier's hold on the fox.

Forming a basic mixture of elements, I slid it into the gargoyle. As I expected, I had to adjust the elements immediately. The purifier's braid of fire and earth had warped the fox's insides, and it was pulling her apart. I wasted precious seconds trying to sever the braid where it tunneled into the gargoyle's neck. The massive bands of elemental energy were too strong for me, so I switched tactics. Laying my hands on her wings, I drove my magic deep into the gargoyle, hunting for the tip of the purifier's magic where it anchored to her body. If I couldn't cut the purifier off before it entered her, maybe I could stop it from digging any deeper.

I found the end of the braid less than two inches from the gargoyle's opposite side. The purifier's magic twisted and churned inside the gargoyle, corkscrewing her innards and creating a rift inside her as if she were just another rock, not a living creature. Only her innate magic bound into her tigereye body kept her alive, and it was failing.

While I examined it, the braid of fire and earth tunneled through another half inch of her body. It wasn't anchored in her; it was boring through her! If it managed to push out her other side, it'd shatter her body.

Knowing I had mere minutes to save her life, I gathered counterelements—water and wood—and threw them against the fire and earth of the purifier. I anticipated the backlash of pain that resonated into me, and I didn't let up. The forward progress of the braid halted; then it began to swell inside the gargoyle, opening physical fractures.

Cursing, I released my countermagic and grabbed quartz-tuned earth. As fast as I could, I healed the fresh wounds; then I shifted my focus to the fox's neck. The divisive magic of the purifier had polarized the magic inside the gargoyle, and I patched the large fractures just under her skin, hoping it would thwart the purifier. Undeterred, the fire and earth braid passed seamlessly through my magic and continued to burrow into the gargoyle.

While I wrecked my brain for a solution, I countered as much of the purifier's advancement as I dared. Anything more would have injured the fox.

I couldn't form an inverted pentagram in front of the purifier's braid as I'd done with the marmot. For starters, I didn't have a convenient quartz crystal to embed the pentagram in or glass loop to contain the bulk of the purifier. The braid was also exponentially larger than before, and without the combined magic of the full spectrums at my disposal, I doubted I could create a pentagram large enough to absorb the incoming fire and earth elements. Furthermore, though no one had confirmed it, I was pretty sure my inverted pentagrams around the marmot were strengthening the purifier, and I didn't want to give this monstrosity any more power.

At a loss, I did the one thing I knew how to do: I healed the gargoyle.

Splitting my attention, I sewed minute quartz stitches deep inside the fox, bridging the dichotomous elements tearing her apart. While she continued to resonate with earth on one side and fire on the other, the divided elements no longer physically split her. It was probably wishful thinking, but I thought her faint life signs might have strengthened, too.

I'd patched up the gargoyle from her neck almost to her hip before I realized why the purifier's magic wasn't interfering with my healing: It didn't fight or overpower my gargoyle-tuned magic because it recognized it as part of the weave.

"She tuned the purifier to gargoyles."

"What does that mean?" Marcus asked.

I glanced up to where he perched on the top boulder, standing on the narrow peak of rock as if it were solid ground. The sight of him that high made my legs feel funny.

"I think there's a gargoyle at the end of every purifier line, feeding it magic."

"Shit."

Elsa hadn't just embedded her original contraption to the marmot gargoyle through the quartz; she'd tuned the magic to feed off the gargoyle. And when the purifier had exploded, it'd still been tuned to lock on to gargoyles. That's why the fire–earth braid ended here, with the fox, while the other four braids stretched out of sight. They'd locked on to the closest gargoyles in their paths, and all the others were outside the park.

I had no way of knowing how far away the gargoyles were, either. I was almost certain this fox had been dormant before the purifier wreaked havoc on her. Otherwise she wouldn't have remained in the park when everyone else evacuated. Were the other trapped gargoyles dormant, too? How many dormant gargoyles existed in the city? Was it an epidemic? Why hadn't I known about them? I didn't deserve the title of gargoyle healer—

Oliver landed heavily next to Marcus, claws digging into the boulder, and the sight of him snapped me out of my self-recriminations. His long body drooped beneath heavy wings, tail limp. Sunlight sat heavy on his dull red-orange scales where normally it glistened, and he was breathing so fast it had to hurt.

"You're okay?" he asked.

"I'm okay."

There wasn't enough room for him on the small landing with me and the fox gargoyle; otherwise I thought he would have climbed down. He settled for reaching one stubby leg toward me. I lifted my hand to rest it on his paw, then immediately jerked it back. He wasn't dull from fatigue; his entire body had been scratched a thousand times over. The sand. He'd been scoured in the sandstorm when he'd flown through the air section.

"Does it hurt?" I asked even as I slid my magic into him.

"Not much."

He lied. It felt as if someone had taken sandpaper to his skin. He stung from the tip of his nose to his tail, more so along his wings. Internally, his body rioted in a nauseating imbalance. Using so much pure air to fly had altered his internal systems far worse than if he'd helped me work exclusively with air magic for weeks.

"Feed from me," I ordered. Seeing Marcus beside him wielding a hefty amount of water, I added, "Feed from both of us." I followed the direction of Marcus's magic and saw he'd linked with Winnigan. The red-haired water elemental stood at the base of the boulders, and together the two full spectrums pummeled the polarized fire section with water.

Magic blossomed inside me, opening a wellspring of strength that more than doubled the amount of elements I could hold.

"Good." I could feel his body begin to stabilize, but I still experienced an echo of the pain of each breath stretching his chapped sides.

Wishing I had more time *and* my bag of seed crystals—a gargoyle healer staple, I'd learned—I fanned fire in gentle waves across the carnelian just beneath the scratched outer layer of Oliver's skin, taking special care around his muzzle and eyelids. My patchwork healing sped his natural regeneration on the worst of his wounded flesh, coaxing his skin to grow fractionally. Oliver shuddered, then stilled as I worked, and I stopped after less than a minute and well before he was fully healed.

"I'm sorry. I have to—"

"Help her," Oliver said, finishing my sentence. He opened his glowing eyes to study the fox gargoyle. "Is she . . . dormant, too?"

"I think so. Whatever you do, don't get close. The purifier is tuned to gargoyles. It might jump to you." I knelt by the fox and slid magic back into her. My quartz stitches were holding, but they weren't doing anything to balance the energy within the gargoyle. Half of her body swirled with fire magic, the other with earth, and her body thrummed with a constant, cramping pain that alternated between her left and right sides.

The leading edge of the polarized energy inside the fox broke through the skin at her hip and shot toward Oliver.

"No!"

I sliced the feeble strands, shocked when my desperate ploy worked and the polarized magic broke and disintegrated.

"Oliver, you've got to get out of here." I tried to close the braid's exit wound on the fox's side, but the moment the braid became trapped inside her, it started swelling, crushing her insides.

"I can't hold it inside her. It'll kill her. You have to go. Get out of the park. Out of the city."

"What will happen to her?" Oliver asked. He hadn't moved, and I hacked through two new shafts of the purifier's magic as they speared toward him.

"I'll save her. She's going to be fine as long as the magic doesn't build up inside her. Which is why you have to leave. I can't keep holding it back."

"Where will that magic go if I leave?" Oliver asked.

"Out. It'll go out."

"To another gargoyle?"

Yes. But not to *my* gargoyle. I couldn't say that out loud, though. "Oliver, please. Go. I need to concentrate."

With an unreadable look, Oliver launched from the rock and disappeared. Praying he didn't stop flying until he reached the edge of Terra Haven, I turned back to the fox gargoyle.

Larger and larger bands of Elsa's hideous polarizing braid escaped from the gargoyle's hip. Dividing my focus, I slid a feeler into the fox and continued to hack and slice any escaping magic. My patches held despite greater amounts of fire and earth feeding into and out of the gargoyle. The purifier showed no signs of weakening.

I no longer nursed the marginal hope that the river would stop the expansion of the polarized magic. Winnigan's earlier prediction of the bubble swallowing the city seemed more plausible, and when it did, the divided magic would decimate Terra Haven and any living creatures in its path. Everything in the wood section would erode; everything in the water section would drown. The air section would choke everything with dust and erode anything left standing. The earth would tear apart homes and offices; the fire would consume anything in its path.

A wall of heat pressed against my back and sweat dripped down my nose, but the polarized magic escaping the fox grew stronger each time I cut it, and I couldn't spare an ounce of concentration to blot my face.

"We've got to move," Marcus said, suddenly standing beside me.

"It'll swallow the gargoyle," I said, glancing up. The wall of polarized magic pushed close enough to touch.

"And us, too. It was hard enough getting out the first time." He grabbed my arm.

"Wait." I fumbled to assemble fresh quartz patches and stitch them into place where the purifier cut into and out of the gargoyle. The polarized magic slid through my elemental bandages as easily as it did through the fox, but my magic might lessen her pain.

I slashed through a helix of fire larger than the fox as Marcus lifted me. Air exploded from my lungs when my stomach crashed down on top of Marcus's shoulder; then he leapt from the pile of boulders to the ground ten feet below.

I tried to scream, but without air, no sound came out. His thick arm held my legs as I jounced helplessly when he landed. He set me on my feet and I whirled to check the fox, but the tall rocks hid her from sight.

Seconds later, the fire–earth braid burst over the rock, and the polarized field swallowed the boulders where we'd been standing. Marcus grabbed my arm and propelled me up the hill to safety, but my eyes were riveted on the gargoyle-tuned braid.

A sinuous shadow intercepted the braid as it shot straight as an arrow across the ground toward the city.

"Oliver! No!"

The young gargoyle dove into the purifier's questing magic, and it burrowed into him, slamming him to the ground.

7

"Oliver!" I flung myself toward his crumpled form, falling over my own feet when they couldn't keep up. My magic reached him first, and I drove it into him and slashed the purifier's twisted weave. Unlike the other two gargoyles, Oliver fought back with me, and our combined magical assault pushed the insidious braid from him. Immediately, it dove back into his chest.

"We need to roll him. I'll push the magic out of him and then we'll get him free of its path."

"No." The weak protest came from Oliver. He couldn't move; the braid had paralyzed him, and continuing to fight off its intrusion left him no strength to move his limbs, but he managed a few words. "Me, not others," he rasped.

Oliver, not another gargoyle. He didn't want me to spare him just to sacrifice another gargoyle.

"No. Not you." I bounced the purifier's strands from Oliver before they could take root. "You're young. I don't know if you have the strength."

"You'll save me."

My chest caved in at his trusting look. Then Oliver closed his eyes to concentrate on fighting the purifier's intrusive magic. No matter how many times we thrust it from him, cut it off before it could enter him, or tried to blockade against it, the strong braid plowed back into Oliver's chest.

All our actions were a stopgap measure. Eventually we'd tire and the purifier would take root in Oliver. It'd divide him just as it had the fox gargoyle, and it'd tunnel through him with the same ruthlessness, only to jump to the next gargoyle.

The polarization field crept closer. What would happen when it reached Oliver? I couldn't abandon him. I couldn't leave him to face the pain and terror alone and paralyzed.

I swiped tears from my cheeks.

Two bundles of elemental energy wrapped in air rocketed over the top of the bubble and dropped beside Marcus and Winnigan. The outer layers peeled back, revealing twin images of Captain Monaghan. He looked as if he stood underwater, his image reflected in the wavy lines of thin water layers.

"Status report," both captains barked, their voices crystal clear.

"We're together and linked," Winnigan said. She hadn't halted her assault on the fire section even as we'd retreated; she'd merely changed tactics, sending crushing waves of water and wood into the braid that attacked Oliver—with minimal results. Speaking and wielding massive amounts of complex magic didn't appear to challenge her.

"That explains the echo," Grant said. One of the mirror spheres disintegrated. The remaining floating head moved, spinning until the captain looked at me. "Good. Oliver found— Crap. Is the purifier connected to him?"

"Elsa tuned the purifier to gargoyles," I said.

"That means there are five gargoyles feeding this thing?"

"We think so," Marcus said. "I think that's what broke the ward around the park. This fire–earth line already overwhelmed one gargoyle. We weren't fast enough to save it. Then it jumped to Oliver."

"Oliver jumped into it," I said.

"Why would he do that?" Grant asked.

"To save another gargoyle." I slashed at the evil burrowing magic, pushing it out of Oliver. The small dragon balanced the disruption to his internal magic, but the fire and earth braid forced its way back into him before he had normalized. I blocked it with swift strokes of wood and water.

"Mika's keeping the purifier from taking root, but she won't last much longer," Marcus said. I gritted my teeth. It was the truth, but I didn't appreciate hearing it.

"It seems to be helping," Winnigan said. "Velasquez and I have been throwing everything we've got at the fire section, trying to weaken it, but I don't think it's made a difference, Captain. Mika preventing the purifier from feeding off Oliver has done more to slow the tide than anything we've done."

Really? I checked the polarization field. It had swallowed the boulders where the fox gargoyle lay trapped, but it hadn't advanced more than a foot up the hill beyond it.

"Marciano and I tried the same thing against wood with similar results. We're going about this wrong. We need to use this freakish magic against itself."

"A destructive pentagram?" Winnigan asked. "How are we going to get a mix of elements through this field?"

"Any way we can. Link up."

A massive bundle of elements shot from Winnigan and flew out of sight over the curve of the polarization field. I watched it go in amazement. A thousand yards had to separate us from the captain, yet these full spectrums acted like linking across such a huge distance was nothing new. For a woman who was proud of being able to work earth a mere five yards away from her, what they did seemed incredible. Seconds later, the magic swelled in Winnigan and Marcus, proving they'd made their connection with Grant and Marciano.

"You, too, Mika," the captain said. "We need a full five for this."

What they needed were five elementals with full spectrums, not four full spectrums and a midlevel earth elemental. I glanced back up the trail toward the tunnel, hoping to catch sight of Seradon returning, fully healed.

"I need to stay focused on Oliver."

"You need to multitask."

I glared at the mirror sphere. "If I stop, even for a minute, it's going to take root. And if it does, this whole field is going to get stronger." And Oliver would be trapped.

"If you don't link up, it won't matter. The field is getting stronger with or without Oliver's contribution. If we want to stop it, we have to work together."

"You can still protect Oliver after you're linked," Marcus said.

I remembered how easily the squad had yanked control from me when I'd been working to save the marmot. This time, they wouldn't be controlling a small containment ward. They would be creating an acre-size pentagram through the polarized magic. That seemed like it would take everything we had and then some. How much magic would I have left to use to keep Oliver safe?

I shifted to sit beside Oliver, laying a hand on a patch of wing I'd healed. Four other gargoyles were trapped throughout the city, and by focusing all my efforts on saving Oliver, they were suffering, slowly being torn apart. I was delaying because I didn't want to see *my* gargoyle hurt, and that wasn't fair to the rest—or to the fox and marmot already engulfed in the polarization field.

"Some party this turned out to be," I grumbled, trying to sound brave.

Winnigan looked at me like I was crazy, but Marcus grinned.

"That's the spirit," he said.

"Winnigan, fan out," Grant said. "This'll be easier if we're not so far apart."

"Right. Let's destroy this monster." Winnigan ceased her water-focused onslaught, clapped Marcus on the shoulder, and jogged back toward the water section. The pond Winnigan and Seradon had swam through less than a half hour ago now spanned the entire polarized wedge, accelerating the erosion in the neighboring wood section. A hundred yards remained between the river and the leading edge of the polarization field, but the spontaneous lake would soon bridge the intervening land. We were running out of time.

The captain's mirror sphere remained beside Marcus, but from the jostling of Grant's image, I guessed he was running to the air section.

The polarization field pulsed, and the moment the braid connected with Oliver, it inched toward us. Oliver fought back, but his efforts weren't as effective as mine.

I bent forward to whisper into Oliver's ear. "Don't give

up. I'm going to be right here, fighting for you. And for all the gargoyles. We're going to free you, but you have to fight it with me."

"All you have to do is link with me; I'll do the rest," Marcus said. He squatted in front of me.

I slashed through the baneful braid, temporarily freeing Oliver, then forced myself to pause long enough to gather a balance of elements and thrust them to Marcus. For a second, I could feel only the two of us, and the power radiating from Marcus wrapped me in comforting warmth. Then he dropped open the barrier between us and the rest of the squad.

I fell into the pool of linked magic and unraveled.

The elements buffeted me, shaving away bits of my identity until I couldn't tell where my body sat or what held me together. Panicking, I flailed for control. The elements flowed around me, cocooned me, battered me, but I couldn't hold a single strand. I was part of the magic, fluid and shifting. Drowning.

"Open your eyes."

Seradon must have held me together last time. She'd buffered me through the whole process, not just when the purifier had exploded.

Damn it, I had no business working with these people. Every one of them was three times as strong as me and mountains more talented. I couldn't even find myself in the link. I was alone. Lost. Where was my body? Where was *I*?

"Look at me."

Marcus's harsh growl rumbled against my eardrums. My body shook, and the movement pulled me back to myself with a snap. I opened my eyes.

The fire elemental held both of my shoulders in

crushing grips, and he jostled me again, snapping my head back and forth.

"Are you with me?"

I nodded when I couldn't find my voice. Two of me were here: one looking into his eyes, the other floating in a conglomeration of magic.

Thinking about the link widened the rift between my two selves, pulling me back into the nebulous expanse of elements. I grabbed Marcus's forearms and squeezed, using the tactile sensation to ground myself.

"You have to hold yourself separate. You're a part of the link, but you're not *the* link. Think about what makes you, you."

What made me, me? I'd never had to think about it. I just was me.

"How?" I croaked. "Can't you just . . ." I hunted for the right word. "Isolate me? Like Seradon did?" Every second of delay cost Oliver and strengthened the purifier. We didn't have time to teach me fancy tricks. I needed to get back into Oliver to protect him.

"If you're going to be any use, you have to be in control of yourself. Focus." His serious lapis lazuli eyes bore into mine. "You're an earther."

Yes. I was an earth elemental. I tested the thought, and all the earth available to me through the link tumbled into me, burying me.

Marcus shook me. "You're a gargoyle healer."

Earth magic refined to quartz at my thought, snapping into a shape I could use to heal gargoyles. I held the thick elemental band separate from myself without falling into it. Progress. The resonance of four powerful people on the other end of the magic jarred me, but I clung to my identity. I was a gargoyle healer, an earth elemental with a specialty in quartz—

In the middle of a magic catastrophe that required the skills of someone far more talented than me.

Doubt and fear separated me another step from the link. The fate of Terra Haven depended on me being the earth elemental in this otherwise competent FPD squad. It was enough to make me want to vomit—a sensation unmatched in the link.

I settled back into my body with a feeling akin to waking. I was me, unique and separate, a part of something larger but not the linked energy itself.

I relaxed my control, and the linked magic swirled through me, pulling me back into the immense mixture of elements. I teetered. *I am a gargoyle healer. I am an earth elemental,* I chanted while watching the bubble of polarized magic expand. *I am terrified.*

I dropped a hand from Marcus's arm to Oliver, and contact with the gargoyle crystallized the separation between me and the link.

"Okay. I've got this."

Marcus scanned my face, then released me. I let go of his other arm and flexed my fingers. My knuckles popped. I'd probably left bruises.

Turning back to Oliver, I peeled a slice of magic from the link and cut the purifier's braid. It resisted and when I added more countermagic, rather than severing the intrusive magic from Oliver, my elements sliced into him. I jerked back and hastily patched the wounds, murmuring an apology to the unresponsive gargoyle. More gently, I countered the fire and earth, pushing the purifier back as far as I dared. It clung to his chest an inch under his skin, rooted in his stone flesh. The time it'd taken me to orient myself in the link had cost Oliver his chance at freedom. If

I'd made the wrong call, I'd doomed Oliver to unending pain.

"Settled?" Grant asked. I jumped, having forgotten about the mirror sphere floating beside me.

"Yes." Tears blurred my vision.

"Good. I need an anchor of solid quartz."

"Really?" Surely they had a better anchoring system for pentagrams.

"Unless you can create a wind funnel in the ground."

I glanced at Marcus in confusion.

"Seradon usually makes our anchors," he said. "She can reshape the earth to harness our elements' strengths: a miniature wind funnel for air, a molten pit for fire, that sort of thing."

Oh. Right. Seradon could do things with earth I only dreamed might be possible. The captain had asked me for quartz because it was what I did best. "Where do you need it?"

It took precious minutes to pinpoint *over here*. With Marcus instructing me through the process, I located Grant standing in front of the expanding air section. Distinguishing the captain from the vat of magic required recognizing his signature, which Marcus described as a cold firestorm but to me looked and felt like the leading edge of a thundercloud, a harnessed forefront of natural violence. After I pinpointed the captain, making the anchor at his feet was easy. With all the magic of the squad at my fingertips, I quested into the soil and yanked a vein of quartz to the surface. A few modifications removed the flaws from the quartz, and I molded it into a head-size sphere.

"That'll work," Grant said. His magic slid into the quartz. In less time than it'd taken me to separate the quartz from the surrounding rock, Grant wove a constructive pentagram, anchored it in the quartz, and grafted a powerful band of air to it. He shot the air straight through the polarized sphere, bisecting the wood section and angling for the apex of the water section.

The impressive display of power would have been distracting under different circumstances, but I had Oliver to worry about. I yanked my awareness back to my body and worked to combat the creep of the purifier's magic into Oliver. It had rooted deeper into the gargoyle while my attention had been elsewhere, doubling his pain.

"Hang in there," I whispered.

"Place another anchor *there*, Mika," Grant ordered through the mirror sphere.

Finding the indicated location was easier this time: I simply followed the straight band of air Grant had created to a distance beyond the center of the water section's arc. The selected location happened to be underwater, but that didn't matter. I reached into the earth below and drew out more schist, then refined a tall finger of quartz to protrude above the waterline. A cool, smooth presence in the link locked on to the new anchor. Winnigan. She built a constructive pentagram into the quartz just as Grant's air element slammed into the anchor, and she deftly wrapped the incoming magic into the quartz, locking it in place. One branch of the pentagram was set.

I switched back to fighting the purifier's encroaching tendrils in Oliver and didn't look up until Marcus called my name. When I did, I felt the strain in the link as Grant shoved raw water magic across the wedge of purified earth and out through the fire section. Setting the air line had been relatively easy; both the wood and water sections contained plenty of physical air to bolster Grant's magic. But shoving water through the damming energy of earth and then through the dry fire section taxed the considerable strength of all the squad. Grant had almost forced his way free of the polarized field, but at this rate, we wouldn't have enough power to finish the last three lines of the pentagram.

"Watch, Mika," Marcus said.

He reached into the polarized fire section and shaped a funnel of fire around Grant's line of water, softening the heat and molding a pathway for the captain. The line of water surged to punch through the polarization field.

"Now you," Marcus said.

"Anchor first," Grant barked.

I'd barely finished forming the quartz outside the fire section when Marcus and Grant took hold of the crystal. Marcus shaped a pentagram, Grant slammed the water into the anchor, and Marcus locked the second line of the pentagram in place.

"Wrap the water with earth, Mika," Marcus said. "Buffer it. We need to free magic for the next line."

I grunted, too busy countering the fire and earth braid in Oliver to respond. He was weakening, and I did my best to shore up his strength even as I fought the burrowing magic.

"Now, Healer," Grant ordered.

"Just a minute."

"*Now!*"

With a snarl, I forced my attention from Oliver. Mimicking Marcus's tunnel, I spun earth around the line of water. I hadn't compensated for my strength when working the purified earth inside the purifier's sphere, and the ground leapt upward into a rock tunnel through which the water magic slid unchallenged.

"Nice," Marcus said in approval.

I barely heard him, having returned to protecting Oliver. Only now I had to split my attention between maintaining the earthen tunnel and fighting the malicious braid. Oliver fought, too, but he couldn't prevent the braid from dividing his internal magic. Already, fire swirled on his right, earth on his left, and the unnatural divide sapped his strength. Every task that forced my attention from Oliver enabled the purifier to bore farther into him, and I despaired at the increasing difficulty of battling the mindless magic. Worse, the magic in the link was dwindling. Winnigan required a chunk to lock the incoming air and outgoing water lines to the anchor in her section, and Marcus required twice as much to lock down the incoming water and outgoing fire lines as well as maintain his protection around the water line inside the polarized fire wedge. On top of that, the captain required the majority of our linked magic to build the remaining lines.

I jumped ahead of Grant to build a quartz anchor at the apex of the wood section and Marciano lashed the incoming fire element to his anchor. Not stopping, Grant plowed a wood line across the wood and water sections toward us. I built the last anchor a few feet to my left, in front of the earth section, but before I could turn back to Oliver, Grant thrust rough-hewn wood magic across the earth section, and I had to scramble to build a new tunnel through the rocks all the way to the anchor to protect his magic. At the last second, I remembered to make a constructive pentagram in the quartz anchor.

"Brace yourself," Marcus said.

The wood magic slammed into the anchor and me at the same time as the captain transferred control to me. I fumbled to grab the fraying ends of the wood line and wrap it into my constructive pentagram inside the quartz. Grant gave me barely enough time to lock it in place before he shoved a fresh band of earth through the anchor. I held tight as Grant shot the final line of the pentagram across the park toward his air anchor.

Magic pulled me in four directions at once, and when I reached for Oliver, all the pieces I held started to unravel.

"Hold it!" Marcus said.

I lurched for the anchor, squeezing the wood and earth lines back into place, only to have my earth tunnels crumble. The entire pentagram trembled under the strain as I righted my fortifications.

"Just a little longer."

My world narrowed to holding my four pieces of magic. If I failed, the pentagram would collapse, the purifier would continue to grow, and Oliver would die.

I shook with the need to get back to defending Oliver.

Marcus said something, but his words garbled against my anxiety. The braid tunneling into Oliver had thickened to span his chest. Without magic, I couldn't tell how far through him it'd burrowed, or how much damage it had done. If I didn't mend the rifts of the dichotomous magic, he'd be torn apart.

Magic blossomed through the link, doubling its strength. I gasped, looking around for what I already knew I'd find.

Gargoyles! We had help!

I spotted four winged shapes against the bright sky and my heart soared.

Through the link, I felt everyone shore up their defenses. Grant connected the earth line to his anchor and a surge of power swept through the five overlapping lines. Yet even with the influx of magic, when I attempted to split a fifth layer of magic toward Oliver, the four others I held quaked.

Far too slowly, the captain took control of the anchors,

and when he had mine, I spun immediately for Oliver. The purifier had burrowed more than halfway through him, and I fought it back with precise ferocity, looking up only once I'd reduced the purifier's magic to the weakest hold possible.

I saw Kylie first. Her white-blond hair streamed behind her as she ran down the hill at Seradon's side. The crack of rock feet landing on granite announced the arrival of the gargoyles. Not just any gargoyles, either. *My* gargoyles.

Oliver's four siblings landed in a semicircle around him, and my heart sank to my toes.

"Back up! Get away from Oliver." I shooed them with a frantic arm, and they hopped aside, Herbert jerking back when I almost bopped his toucan nose. "This isn't safe. What are you doing here?"

"We had to come. You need us," Anya said.

An outsider would never guess the five adolescent gargoyles had been born in the same clutch. Quinn looked like a small citrine lion with the scales of a dragon instead of fur; Anya resembled a panther, though one with a navy dumortierite and mint-green aventurine body rather than black; Lydia's purple, pink, and orange agate swanlike body glowed like a flying sunset; and Herbert's pink quartz armadillo body and toucan beak were shot through with cobalt dumortierite. Aside from Lydia's two lionlike feet vaguely resembling Quinn's, no two siblings shared the same animal characteristics—other than wings, of course, but all gargoyles had wings.

"Is Oliver okay?" Quinn asked, creeping closer again.

"No." I fought the purifier's magic even as I waved him back.

"Whoa! What happened to the park?" Kylie asked as she pounded to a stop near us.

"Sir, I'm back with reinforcements," Seradon said, speaking to the captain's mirror sphere.

"Hold tight. I'm going to loose the destructive magic." Grant's sphere flickered and disintegrated.

"Grant!" Kylie cried.

"Hush. He's fine," Seradon said, grabbing Kylie's arm and holding her in place without looking away from the park.

A perfect half-sphere of polarized magic cupped the middle two-thirds of the park, transforming the once beautiful terrain into five nightmarish wedges of destruction. Thick lines of the largest pentagram ever created inside the bounds of Terra Haven bisected the dome, the five quartz anchors at the pentagram's points now barely two feet from the leading edge of the creeping magic. Ignoring all normal laws of magic, four bands of looping elemental pairings speared arrow-straight across the undulating grounds and disappeared into the city. The fifth bore into Oliver.

Grant stabilized the magic flowing through the enormous park-spanning pentagram. Drawing on the boost of magic from the gargoyles, he fortified the bonds connecting each tip of the pentagram, then freed them from the anchors.

The pentagram shrank until the tips rested against the underside of the purifier's sphere. I held my breath.

"Come on," Seradon said. "Work, damn it."

Magic surged through the pentagram as each element branch drank from the polarized magic on one end and destroyed it on the other, using the purifier's magic against itself.

The polarization field shrank, slowly at first, then faster, retreating in a rush toward the center of the park and the marmot gargoyle where it all began. A wave of heat escaping the fire section washed over us, whipping my ponytail against the side of my face and drying the sweat in my scalp. The incessant rumble and cracks of earth died down, and the snap of tree branches and the muted roar of the new waterfall filled in the silence.

My relieved sigh caught in my throat when I reached for Oliver. Magic gushed from him, the thick braid sucking down his life as fast as the pentagram destroyed the purifier's polarized magic. The traumatic drain ripped fissures through Oliver's insides, and pain fractured my skull, an echo of the agony Oliver experienced.

I tried to stop the purifier from feasting on his magic, but it was too strong. My only option was to hack the braid from him, inflicting more cuts into his tortured body to sever its tendrils. When I sliced the last of the fire and earth strands from his chest, the braid snapped toward the dwindling dome of polarized magic, its slingshot speeds unchanged when it passed through the fox gargoyle.

The moment I freed Oliver, I wove patches through his body, mending all the cuts and evening his internal magic with gentle brushes of magic. I didn't let up until he'd stabilized, and then only because I didn't want to add too much strain to his body.

He opened his eyes, blinking up at me, and even managed a small smile.

"We did it. You're going to be okay," I said.

"The other lines aren't retreating," Kylie said, pointing to the four remaining braids stretching beyond the horizon. At the center of the park, the dome of polarized magic shrank out of sight.

"Oh no," Seradon said.

The other gargoyles. They didn't have a healer on hand

to cut the braids from them. The destruction of the purifier would drain the magic from them and kill them.

"I've got to help them!"

I sprang to my feet. I needed transportation. A pegasus or gryphon or flying carpet, something fast and—

The severed fire–earth braid rebounded, hurtling up the slope on its previous trajectory. I lunged for Oliver, but it reached him first, burrowing back into his chest with renewed vigor.

8

⊘⊛⊗⊘⊘

Oliver whimpered and stilled. I fell to my knees, fighting cable-thick bands of fire and earth. Through sheer will and with the backing of all the power of the link, I forced the purifier's braid from Oliver. It wormed back into him the moment I slackened my defense.

Seradon crouched and examined Oliver. "She tuned it to gargoyles," she said, recognizing the problem instantly. "Damn that woman!"

A dome of polarized magic sprang to life at the heart of the park, then swelled with alarming speed as the five divided elements rebuilt. Thanks to the earlier remodeling of the park, each section was sculpted to support a singular element and all the counterelements had already been eliminated.

Grant yanked magic through the link, setting fire to the overgrown groves in the botanical gardens and funneling water across the park to the fire section through a huge trough he cut into the earth in front of the expanding polarization bubble. The field stuttered as it battled destructive elements, its expansion reduced to a slow creep. The captain had bought us time, but not much.

A new mirror sphere rocketed across the park and opened in front of Marcus.

"This isn't going to work until we can disconnect the gargoyles," Grant said.

Everyone turned to look at me. When Grant spotted Kylie behind me, his face tightened, but he didn't say anything.

"I don't know if I can," I said, keeping up a steady counterattack on the purifier's braid in Oliver. Quinn crept closer to his brother on almost silent rock paws, and I shooed him back again.

"We don't know how far away they are," Marcus said, eyes on the horizon. The water–earth purifier line extended across Lincoln River and disappeared into the city beyond. The others looked equally long.

"It's not just the distance," I said. "Even if I could reach them all, I don't think I could break the purifier's connection. Once it gets a firm hold, I can't force it out without tearing the gargoyle apart. All I could do for the fox was patch her insides so the magic didn't kill her."

"The fox?" Seradon asked.

"Another gargoyle was connected to this line, there, in the rocks," I said, pointing. I wished I could get back to the fox now and check on her, but until the purifier was destroyed, I wasn't leaving Oliver's side. "This corrosive braid channeled through her."

"Then it jumped to Oliver?" she asked.

"In a way. He put himself in its path. It would have kept going until it found another gargoyle. Oliver thought . . ." He thought I could save him, and I was doing a miserable job. "I'm barely staying ahead of the braid in him."

"I see that," Grant said.

Of course. Through the link, he'd know exactly how I fought the purifier in Oliver, just as I knew he continued to feed fire into the trees across the park, drawing on magic from the link. A huge column of smoke rose into the sky, matched in the fire section where the captain's river of water doused flames and molten embers alike.

"If it bore through the fox that quickly, the other lines might have already slid through the first gargoyles they encountered and be on to the next," Seradon said.

I felt sick. *Slid* didn't come close to describing what would have happened to those gargoyles. Without my patches to hold them together, the dual polarized magic would have shattered their bodies, killing them before embedding itself in the next victim.

"So you can break the purifier lines from the next gargoyles before they have a chance to take root?" Grant phrased it as much as an order as a question.

"Maybe." If I was close to the gargoyle. If the timing was just right. If I let the four currently trapped gargoyles die first.

"We couldn't link that far apart," Marcus said. "Even if Mika broke one or two of the purifier's lines, she wouldn't be able to hold them from all five gargoyles at once over that distance, either."

"She might not need to. We could each take a gargoyle and defend it after she's broken the purifier's hold," Winnigan said, her voice faint through Grant's mirror sphere. He must have a similar sphere next to Winnigan and Marciano, conferencing us all into this conversation.

"That's some complex quartz manipulation she's doing," Seradon said. "Look at how she's holding Oliver together while countering the purifier. She's perpetually healing and fighting at the same time. Do you think you could do that?"

I didn't know who she directed her question toward, but I couldn't believe she doubted her teammates. They could do mind-boggling things with the elements; surely they could work quartz at this scale.

"Maybe. No. Not like that." Marcus squinted at my weaves. "But if the purifier wasn't embedded in the gargoyle and I only had to hold it back, I could do that."

Grant shook his head. "No. Seradon's right. We need the gargoyles to be closer. Can we move them?"

"That'd take time," Marcus said.

"It might be our only option."

"We could hold the lines closer," Anya said.

"What? No!" I whirled to face the gargoyle. She flared her wings at my outburst. Seated next to Oliver, I was marginally taller than the blue and green panther. When I'd first met her, she'd been barely as large as a housecat, but she'd always possessed the same determined look when she made up her mind.

"Let her speak," Grant said.

"No." Anya was proposing likely suicide for her and her siblings. It was bad enough Oliver was suffering through the purifier's attack.

"My siblings and I could hold the divisive braids here, close enough for Mika to reach." Anya glanced at her siblings, and they all nodded in complete agreement. I bit off another protest. "Mika would be able to keep them from burrowing into us as she's doing with Oliver."

Fight this same battle on five fronts against five different elemental braids of polarizing magic? Even with the full power of the link behind me, I doubted it was possible.

"If I fail, you'll all be trapped. You might die." It was hard to force the words out, but Anya needed to know.

The gargoyle panther shook her head. "You will protect us."

"I *am* protecting you by telling you not to do this."

"We have to. For Oliver. I know you won't let us die."

I swallowed against a lump in my throat. I didn't deserve that kind of blind trust, but against such unwavering confidence, there wasn't anything I could say to change her mind.

"It might work," Seradon said.

"It *will* work. Mika is strong," Anya said.

"It will only work if the purifier will lock on a closer gargoyle and let go of the one farther away," Grant said.

"I will try," Lydia said. She spread her wings to launch, and I grabbed for her.

"Wait! Let me try something."

I fumbled with the elements, my panic making me clumsy, and I teetered into the vast magic of the link. *I am a gargoyle healer. I am terrified.* The thoughts anchored me.

After pummeling the braid back far enough to give myself a breather, I used a hook of earth to lift a vein of quartz from the soil in front of Oliver. I separated a solid bar of purified quartz from the rest and dropped it onto my palm. Then I shoved the earth smooth again while shaping the quartz into a disk. I made it the exact same size and shape as the disks I'd used to protect the marmot, and I placed it against Oliver's chest. A few layers of the elements and a twist to invert the pentagram, and I had a duplicate blockade.

The purifier's thick magic passed through it as if it didn't exist and burrowed into Oliver.

"It was worth a try," Seradon said.

I wasn't ready to give up. Stripping the quartz of all

elemental magic, I started fresh, feeding it a combination of elements that resonated with gargoyles. If I could make the purifier think the quartz rock was a gargoyle, maybe I could trick it into locking on to a piece of rock instead of a living creature.

This time when I held the disk in front of Oliver, the fire and earth braid reacted, unraveling my magic too fast to follow and pulverizing the quartz to dust before leaping into Oliver.

I slumped even as I blocked the deadly braid. I could tune quartz to harmonize with a gargoyle, but I couldn't infuse the complexity of a living being into the lump of rock to make it strong enough to withstand more than a second of the braid's attack.

Smoke blew into my eyes, and Kylie casually pushed it aside with a brush of air, her magic stronger thanks to the gargoyles. The expanding raw earth stifled the river Winnigan continued to funnel from the newly formed lake along the path Grant had cut, and steam hissed louder than a geyser as the water evaporated in the fire section. Across the park, new green growth smothered the burning trees. It wouldn't be much longer before the purifier's divided magic retook the ground we'd gained and continued its inexorable push toward the city. I couldn't think of any other options to try, and we were running out of time. We had to stop this.

I forced the words through numb lips. "We have to use gargoyles."

Seradon rested her hand on my shoulder, her eyes troubled. "If you can keep the purifier's invasion to a minimum, you'll be able to break them all free. This should work."

If and *should* were not words I wanted to use in tandem with gargoyle lives.

"You'll have to free all the gargoyles simultaneously

when I activate the destructive pentagram again," the captain said. "This is powerful, unpredictable magic. If your timing's off, the backlash could leave you scarred. Or nullified."

Now he tried to talk me out of it?

I slashed the hungry tendrils of fire and earth as they tried to root into Oliver, but my eyes swept over the other four gargoyles. If we didn't give this a try, the city would be consumed and torn apart by the polarized magic. That thought alone should have been enough motivation, but I wasn't thinking about the city. I was thinking about the countless gargoyles who would suffer or die. Out in the city, four other gargoyles were currently being used as amplification tools for the purifier, helplessly being fed upon. They didn't have anyone fighting the purifier for them. My little gargoyles were willing to try to save them, and their bravery humbled me. I didn't relish taking the chance of being mentally scarred; the possibility of being nullified made my hands shake.

"I won't be any help with the pentagram," I said.

"We already laid the ground work. We'll manage without you this time," Grant said.

I turned to Lydia. She cocked her agate head, and when I reached across Oliver, she rubbed against me. "You'll be paralyzed the moment you touch the magic. Don't fly into it."

"Okay." She backed up to give herself room to extend her wings.

"Be careful."

Lydia launched into the air and flew toward the purifier's braid of air and fire on the other side of the fire section. I watched her go with my heart in my throat, wishing I could call her back.

No one spoke as she dropped to the ground a few feet from the thick helix cables flowing out of the park in an unerringly straight line. Lydia examined the braid, her long neck snaking back and forth in agitation; then she flared her wings and dove into the flow of magic.

The instant it touched her, she froze, paralyzed. Polarized air and fire drilled into her body, and I dove in with it. Pain exploded in my mind, almost jostling me from the gargoyle, but I clung to her and threw my magic against the purifier. Earth countered air and water countered fire. Dividing my efforts, I patched Lydia's insides with fresh gargoyle-tuned weaves of quartz, and I didn't let up until the purifier's hold had weakened to mere tendrils. Then I bounced back to Oliver and checked the steady creep of the purifier into his body.

"It worked," Marcus said.

The purifier's braid now ended at Lydia. Whatever gargoyle had previously been pinned on the end of the esurient magic had been freed, leaving Lydia as trapped as Oliver.

"Praise the skies," Grant said in a rare display of emotion.

"Captain," Seradon said. The warning in her tone made me look. The polarization field bulged, consuming three feet of ground in every direction, extinguishing the last of the water in the fire section. A crack and grumble of shifting earth dammed Winnigan's rerouted river.

"Looks like it's going to be a race," Grant said. "The rest of you gargoyles, move out."

"Wait!" I grabbed for Anya, Herbert, and Quinn, and they stumbled to a stop, turning to look at me. "Drop in one at a time around the circle. And fight with everything you've got."

Quinn ran back to me to nuzzle his broad lion head against my arm; then all three were airborne, flying high over the purifier's bubble to sacrifice themselves, secure in their beliefs that I could save them.

————

ANYA FUSED WITH THE PURIFIER FIRST, STEPPING INTO THE line of wood and air between Marciano and Grant. I thought I was prepared for the purifier's swift attack, but it still caught me off guard. For several harrowing minutes, I grappled with the ferocious braid, patching Anya as I could until I forced the purifier *almost* out of her. Then I had to leap to Oliver to fight the encroaching divisive magic in him, then in Lydia, before I could check on Anya again. A few quick snips kept the purifier in place.

I took a steadying breath. I could do this.

"Herbert needs somewhere to land," Seradon said. "Velasquez, build him a platform. Make it strong. If he falls into the water, he might drown before we can save him."

I struggled to focus on the physical world. Where Herbert needed to land between the water and the wood sections, the ground had eroded, and a waterfall cascaded along the purifier's braid. The moment the line touched him, Herbert would be paralyzed and he'd plummet to the bottom of the churning water.

A platform of granite lifted from the ground, growing until it cleared the water by five feet. I felt for the magic creating it, surprised to find more than the cables of earth reshaping the rock—I could distinguish Marcus's magic signature, a steady heat wrapped around a core of rosewood and sparking with lightning like a living jewel. It was a signature as impressive as the man himself. He wasn't half bad with earth, either. I should have expected nothing less from a full spectrum, even if he was a fire elemental. Nevertheless, I wasn't taking any chances with Herbert's life.

Any more *chances,* my guilty conscience accused.

"It needs to be stronger." I twined my magic through Marcus's, reinforcing the granite with a cage made from quartz I located from near the base of the pillar. Nothing short of a fire-fused thunderbolt would break the platform.

"You're getting bossy," Marcus said.

My rebuttal was cut short when Herbert landed on the platform and the purifier's polarized wood and water magic sliced into him. Methodically, I beat it back, layering familiar patches to lessen the pain. His acute agony had barely faded to a dull ache when Quinn fell into the line of water and earth.

"Too fast," I gasped, but he was too far away to hear, and it was too late anyway. The purifier drew strength from all five gargoyles, eating into them. I siphoned magic from the link to combat it on five fronts, frustrated by the lag in the magic. When I tried to grab more, Grant growled.

"Work with what you've got," he said, his voice coming from over my shoulder in the mirror sphere.

I growled right back, too focused on saving Quinn to form words. A giant shaft of air speared between one anchor and the next, consuming the magic in the link as Grant rebuilt the destructive pentagram. The extra boost the four gargoyles had given us had been cut off one by one as they'd sacrificed themselves to the purifier.

I seized all available remaining magic, and even though I wielded more than I could normally hold even when a gargoyle boosted me, it still didn't feel like enough.

As soon as Quinn was safe, I hopped to Oliver, then Lydia,

Anya, Herbert, and back to Quinn. Cycling through the gargoyles wasn't fast enough. The purifier ate into them with mechanical relentlessness, and every time I slowed to fight it out of one gargoyle, it gained a deeper hold on the others.

Dividing my magic, I countered air in Anya and Lydia at once, then shifted to counter fire in Lydia and Oliver. Working my way around the circle fighting the purifier in two gargoyles at once proved more effective, but it still wasn't enough. I split my focus again. Since earth was my strongest element, I kept a steady onslaught of earth against air in Lydia and Anya while countering an additional polarized element in a third gargoyle. Oliver, Quinn, Herbert, and back to Oliver, then to the fire in Lydia, the wood in Anya, and back to Oliver.

I lost all sensation of my body, dizzy inside the magic and unable to slow for even a second to gain my bearings. My world narrowed to the noxious rooting braids and the purifier's unrelenting attack.

"Is she breathing?" Kylie asked. Her words bubbled out of the space between the gargoyles, and I dismissed them. They had nothing to do with saving the gargoyles.

"Don't touch her. Don't break her concentration," Seradon said.

I wouldn't break. I'd shatter. Or disintegrate. I existed in three places at once, fighting three different battles, and every so often, I found a spare thought for a fourth division of magic, and I wove a healing patch in a gargoyle. I was beyond being able to differentiate between them. They were simply five points, five homes for my consciousness. Five pieces of me, and all of them hurt.

The pain echoed through my magic, throbbing aches layered atop sharp stabs in discordant pulses that became my rhythm of movement. Jump to the sharp pain, fight, soothe, move on to the next.

Magic stuttered to me, its strength varied and always less than I needed. The only way I'd get ahead of the purifier was to work faster, and to work faster, I needed more magic.

As if in response to my thought, a rush of magic filled me, and I jounced between the gargoyles so fast it felt as if I touched them all at once.

"I'm ready to activate the pentagram."

The words struck like a gong in my head. I struggled to speak and managed, "Gnnnaaa."

"She's not ready, sir," Seradon interpreted.

"I can see that, but she needs to get ready. Mika, can you hear me? The field is going to overwhelm those gargoyles if you don't free them. Now."

Trying. I'm trying, I thought, but I couldn't get the words out.

With the influx of magic, I reversed my tactics and grabbed a braid, pulling it from one gargoyle—Lydia. Huge coils of air and fire ripped from her chest and writhed in my grip. The elements divided, some seeking a way back into Lydia, some angling over her. Like it had a mind, a predatory consciousness, the purifier's braid hunted for the next life to suck dry. I strained to hold it in check, and it took all my concentration to box in the raw power. I wouldn't be able to hold all five braids until the destructive pentagram destroyed them. Even if I had control of all the magic in our link, it would have been beyond me. As it was, I couldn't even spare enough magic to grab another.

Yet I couldn't make myself release the corrupted magic back into Lydia. She was free, but the moment I let go of the purifier, she'd be pinned and paralyzed again. We'd be right back where we started.

My heart squeezed. Lydia, Anya, Quinn, Herbert, and Oliver had all entrusted me with their lives. If I couldn't break the purifier's hold on *all* of them, they'd die. Because I wasn't the healer they needed me to be.

Unless . . .

Unless the purifier wasn't attached to Lydia. Unless I gave the purifier something else to latch on to.

I had already fractured into pieces. I could feel my five gargoyles more clearly than I could distinguish my body. I felt their pain and their lives as if they were my own. All it would take was a reversal. Not quite a swap. More like a transplant.

I released the air and fire braid, holding it at bay against Lydia's skin, letting it hook into her only enough to prevent it from jumping to a more distant gargoyle.

"Mika. I'm activating the pentagram. We can't wait."

No. I'm not ready.

The purifier's magic trembled, then surged tighter and stronger into the gargoyles, latching on and pulling magic from them as the pentagram drained the magic from the polarization fields.

I flung myself from gargoyle to gargoyle, tearing the purifier's hooks from each one. I didn't try to be gentle, and I forced myself to ignore the wash of pain echoing from them. I focused on myself. Me. The gargoyle healer.

I thought about the link, about how I'd felt when Marcus had coached me through finding myself. I paused my assault long enough to pull myself into one place; then I split my essence again and again into five perfect copies.

"Mika, what are— No! That's a terrible idea," Seradon cried.

My singular connection with the link fractured to five points, and I spun at the end of those points like five kites at the end of cobweb strings. Seradon was wrong. This was the only option, the only way to protect the gargoyles. It might not be the way the FPD squad would do things, but I wasn't part of the squad and I wasn't a full spectrum. I was a gargoyle healer, and I wasn't going to let a gargoyle die, not when I could prevent it.

"Mika, stop!" Marcus bellowed.

I flung myself in five directions, latching each piece of my essence onto a separate gargoyle. Burrowing into them, I reshaped my selves to resonate with each gargoyle.

My body fractured. Knives of pure fire cut through my skull. I screamed, or someone did. Someone felt that pain, but it wasn't me. It wasn't all of me.

My five selves grabbed hold of the purifier in its five different forms and wrapped each in bands of counter-magic. I was pure water and earth fighting fire and air. I was fire and air fighting wood and water. I was all five elemental pairings at once, and I was gargoyle, too. I was quartz and fire and a sprinkling of water and wood and air lifting my wings.

My teeth chattered. I could hear but not feel them clacking together. No, they had to be someone else's teeth. My mouths were closed. My bodies were paralyzed.

The purifier's hold on us weakened. It couldn't pierce our magic. It retreated. Slowly at first, then it suctioned away from us, pulling free of our bodies. We clung to it. If we released it, it would find another gargoyle. It wouldn't stop. Only we could stop it.

The purifier fought us, tried to escape, but we held. We just had to hold.

"Let go, Mika. You've got to let go."

"What did she do?"

"She's going to kill herself."

"Mika! Let GO!"

Marcus's voice boomed against my eardrums. *My* eardrums. I jarred back to the tiny neglected sixth part of my self and snapped my eyes open.

Lapis lazuli eyes filled my blurry vision.

"Can you hear me? Break the link. Let go. Let the pentagram work."

I fractured to pieces, most of me sucking toward the center of the park, pulled by the vortex of destructive magic in Grant's pentagram and the purifier braids to which we— no *I*—clung.

If I released them now, would I survive the backlash? Would I be nullified?

I hesitated, my terror echoing through all the pieces of me.

"Shit, Mika. Break the link. Pull yourself together."

My head jostled on my neck. Marcus was shaking me, and I wanted to tell him to stop. It hurt. All of me hurt. The pain seared through my brain, eating through the cobweb strings. I broke from the purifier and scrambled to reel myself in, but the cobwebs had morphed to razor wires, and each tug sliced through my skull.

My body convulsed in Marcus's grip, the sky spun above me, and my consciousness imploded.

9

W armth unfurled. I hadn't known I was cold until I felt the heat's steady, solid presence. I drifted closer to it, then burrowed into it, pulling it tight around myself. It expanded to cradle me.

An expansive hollowness opened inside me. It should have been terrifying, but I recognized it and the potential it represented. It wasn't love, but it was something close.

A web of elements unfolded around me, each line of magic beckoning. I reached out and tentatively touched one. It hummed like a violin string beneath a bow. I strummed another element, and another. Each resonated through me, reshaping me.

A jagged line of fractured magic pulsed among the elements. I shied away, but the gentle warmth solidified around me, a cocoon of heated rosewood. Emboldened, I reached for the magic around the fracture and carefully knit it back together. Earth and fire and breaths of air made it whole.

I spotted another anomaly, and this time water and air

and earth mended it. Again and again, I repaired the broken magic, bolstered by the solid heat holding me and the familiar hollowness engulfing it.

When I sealed the last fracture, I recognized the hollow sensation. Gargoyle. But not just any gargoyle. Oliver.

The cocoon trembled with my excitement. Oliver was alive. He was boosting me, which meant he wasn't trapped in the purifier. He was safe.

My thoughts tumbled together, and I jolted to full consciousness.

I stared up at Marcus, the hard lines of his face haloed by the clear blue sky. Magic eased from me, taking with it his warmth.

"What happened?" I rasped.

"You were stupid."

"What?" I squinted at those lapis lazuli eyes, then rolled my head to the side. Oliver hunched beside me, his muzzle pressed to my arm. I tried to reach for him, but my fingers only wiggled. Oliver nuzzled me, returning my pathetic attempt at a smile with a grin.

"You divided your spirit—a *very* stupid thing to do," Marcus said, pulling my gaze back to him. "Then in a stroke of sheer idiocy, you anchored each piece separately to another living creature. But that wasn't enough for you. You had to prove you were a master dimwit and you changed your resonance to match the gargoyles'."

"That part was pretty impressive, if astronomically dumb," Seradon said.

"You could have torn your brainless head to shreds with that stunt," Marcus continued, talking over Seradon. "You would have. You would have killed yourself. You would be a splintered null vegetable right now—"

"She doesn't need you to yell at her," Seradon said, stepping into view as she patted Marcus's tense shoulders. "I'm sure her hearing is perfectly fine."

The fire elemental took a deep breath and continued in a rough growl. "You'd be a meat sack right now if your gargoyles hadn't buffered you."

"It took all five," Seradon said. "It was incredible. I didn't know it was possible. They held you inside them. Like they wrapped you in magic. I think it only worked *because* you changed your resonance."

"They're all safe?" I asked.

"Yes, they're all safe," Seradon said.

Relief lifted me from my body. I closed my eyes until the dizziness passed. "If I sit up, are you going to shake me again?" I asked Marcus.

He huffed a breath, then relaxed his grip on my shoulders and helped me up. Stone feet cracked against the granite boulders as Lydia and Quinn landed nearby. Quinn galloped to me, skidding to a stop when Marcus blocked him from barreling into me.

"Are you okay, Mika?" the young gargoyle asked, his goofy lion face scrunched with concern.

"I'm fine." Okay, that was a lie. My head was going to split open if I moved too fast, and my entire body ached. The only part of me that didn't hurt was my left foot, and that was because it was still wrapped in Marcus's field patch.

Lydia snaked her head around Oliver, her glowing purple eyes scanning my body. "The fire elemental is right. That was stupid."

"Lydia!" Kylie scolded. She pushed Marcus aside and knelt in his place. I missed the support of his hands on my shoulders. I hadn't realized how much I'd been leaning on him. It hadn't been just the gargoyles who had saved me. It'd been his warmth, his magic cradling me while I recovered.

"How long was I out?" I asked.

"Five minutes. The longest five minutes of my life, too. You scared the crap out of me." Kylie brushed a wisp of hair from my face with shaking fingers.

"Sorry about that."

"But you did it. You saved Terra Haven."

The way she said it made me groan. She was going to try to make me into a hero again.

"No, *we* did it. Marcus and Grant and Winnigan and Marciano—"

"And you," Kylie insisted.

"And the gargoyles."

The captain's mirror sphere whirled through the air and halted less than a foot from my face.

"I specifically told you to stay out of this, Kylie Grayson. Who let you back in here?" Grant barked.

"And I've told you I answer to the public, not you," Kylie said calmly.

"Journalism does not trump the law."

"Sir, I recruited her," Seradon said.

The mirror sphere shot back several paces so the captain could take in all of us. "Explain."

"I knew you would need help and I figured our healer would have gargoyles who owed her a favor or two. I asked Kylie to contact them for me."

"You called the others?" I asked.

Kylie nodded proudly. I curled my fingers into the rock. She'd meant well, but her rash decision had endangered all my gargoyles' lives.

My swollen finger protested, the pain cutting

temporarily through my headache, and I relaxed my hands. It'd all worked out. Berating Kylie now would be pointless. She couldn't have predicted how dangerous the situation would be for the gargoyles.

"This still doesn't explain why Kylie is back inside the park," Grant said.

"Have you ever tried to argue with a mule?" Seradon asked.

"Hey!" Kylie protested. She had risen to her feet beside Seradon, and the mirror sphere rose with her so it floated well above my head. I let their words wash over me and turned to the gargoyles. I thanked them, knowing my words were inadequate. Quinn burrowed into my left side, and Lydia bustled around Oliver to rest against my thigh. I ran my fingers over their smooth sides—careful of Oliver's rough patches—and it seemed like enough for them. I closed my eyes for a moment, savoring the peace of being surrounded by gargoyles, all of us safe.

"Where are Anya and Herbert?" I asked.

"With the captain," Quinn said. He'd begun to purr, and it garbled his words. A tiny smile cracked my lips.

"How did you recover enough to provide a boost?" I asked Oliver. He'd curled his tail around my back and pressed up against my right side, so close that he had to tilt his head all the way back to look me in the eye. "When you got out of the air section, we hardly had time to balance you, yet you feel stronger than ever."

"I opened myself to your link," he said.

"While you were pinned by the purifier?"

"It was the only way to keep fighting," Lydia said. She ran her beak through the long feathers of a wing, straightening ruffled rock quills.

I reached for the elements, gratified when earth came easily to my call. It was just my strength, no link or gargoyle enhancement, and it'd never been so wonderful to hold such a small amount of magic. I formed a basic test pentagram, refined it to resonate with a gargoyle, and slid it into Oliver. Pain echoed along the link from the laceration made by the purifier. The raw patches on his skin stung and a general soreness soaked his body. None of the injuries were serious, and he would heal from them all with time, but I planned to speed up his recovery. As soon as I felt stronger.

Lydia and Quinn were better off, not having suffered through the sandstorm and having been trapped in the purifier a shorter amount of time.

"You guys are incredible."

"We're heroes. We saved the other gargoyles," Oliver said.

"You saved the whole city. That should be the title of Kylie's next article: 'The Gargoyles Who Saved Terra Haven.'"

Oliver trilled in agreement. I'd have nightmares, but he didn't appear to have any regrets after the traumatic ordeal.

"You like this kind of excitement, don't you?" I asked Oliver.

"Yes."

"Even after everything you went through?"

He shrugged. "We saved lives."

It was the kind of answer I would have expected from a member of the FPD squad.

The wind shifted, bringing with it the dry heat dissipating from the fire section along with an acrid scent of charred earth. If possible, the park looked worse than before. I sought out the rock boulder holding the fox gargoyle, relieved to see it unaffected by the magma bubbling against the base. I'd have to wait to check on the fox until the area cooled. The marmot needed my help, too, as did the other gargoyles who had been trapped at the end of the purifier's braids. But first I had to convince my legs to move.

"Something's wrong," Marcus said. He stood a few feet away on a tall outcropping of rocks, surveying the park. "The magic doesn't feel right."

"Of course not," Seradon said. "It's going to take—"

"Squad. Convene on my signal," Grant barked through the mirror sphere. A shaft of light shot upward from the center of the park, the captain hidden by the landscape.

Marcus hopped down and strode to my side. "Can you stand?"

"Yes." *Maybe.* The gargoyles gave me space and I struggled to get my feet beneath me. Marcus gripped my arm and tugged me upright as if I weighed no more than a doll.

"What about walking?"

"No problem," I said, all bluff. My legs were rubber. I wanted to lie down and take a nap and not wake until the pain in my head abated.

"Maybe you should stay here," Kylie said. "I'll go get a healer. You're in no condition to—"

"No." Grant's tone brooked no argument. "Mika needs to come here."

My heart sank. We weren't linked, and the captain wasn't likely to want to use me in a link again, anyway. A gargoyle had to be in trouble, and from Grant's location, it had to be the marmot.

I took a step. My knees wobbled but didn't collapse.

"I could carry you again," Marcus offered.

"Again?" Kylie echoed.

I was tempted. My foot was still cut, even if I couldn't feel it through Marcus's field wrap. I was exhausted. I hurt. But he had taken injuries, too, and I wasn't going to add to them if I didn't have to. Plus, I was afraid that if I allowed myself a moment of weakness, my remaining willpower—the only thing holding me upright and conscious—would evaporate. The marmot gargoyle needed me; I'd be weak later.

My steps evened out, but Marcus kept a hand under my elbow. I must have looked as bad as I felt if he expected me to collapse at any moment. Quinn, Lydia, and Oliver trailed us for a few feet, then took flight when we started climbing the granite teeth. I would have preferred the flatter ground of the former fire section, but embers smoldering among the magma flow nixed that option. A small lake flooded the water section, and it would have taken too long—and too much energy—to circle around to the air section, where the dust cloud was settling to reveal a sand-blasted landscape a great deal smoother than the one through which we climbed.

Marcus lifted me up taller steps and carried me down the steep descent on the other side. I grumbled my thanks and pretended I'd managed the whole earthen obstacle course on my own. Marcus's lips curled in a small smile. I was doing my best to appear stoic and strong, and he found me amusing. Great.

"Okay. We get it. You're a tough little healer," Seradon said when I paused to catch my breath. She grabbed my left arm and looped it over her shoulders, circling my waist with her right arm. "But it's time to move."

Marcus grinned and lifted my right arm around his shoulders, clutching the waistband of my pants with his left. Between the two of them, my feet touched the ground only every third or fifth step, and we covered the rest of the distance to the central pentagon at a run that somehow left me more winded than either of the squad members. Kylie ran in our wake, and I caught fragments of her panted words as she described the park to herself. I didn't need to look to know she captured her words in a bubble of air that she'd use as notes when she wrote her article.

At the heart of the park, the central pentagon plateau had suffered the most drastic alterations. The ground on the wood side was simply gone. The hole dropped away in a triangular wedge heavily eroded on the right by the air section and on the left by water. The plateau would have been submerged without the outlet the sinkhole provided, judging by the amount of water filling it. A V of ankle-high, razor-thin marble and granite defined the tip of the earth section, ending at the marmot's toes. It cut a ridge straight through the broken marble pentagram, and below the plateau, it dammed the water on the left and the cooling ripples of magma on the right. The ring of sycamore trees around the pentagram had been reduced to two, both with roots submerged in the receding pool. The others had burned or toppled.

The marmot had survived better than I feared. A little water and heat couldn't hurt him. The ground remained stable and flat under his feet. Only his side that had been exposed to the sandstorm had suffered.

But it wasn't my need to heal the raw length of his body that spurred my steps. A sphere encased the marmot, and the elements swirled around the outside like the rainbow on a bubble of soap, only this bubble was twice my height and equally as wide. Inside, the elements simply didn't exist.

Grant, Winnigan, and Marciano stood to one side, and above them, Herbert and Anya perched on the same pillar where Oliver had sat hours earlier when we'd first arrived.

Short-lived relief flashed through me at the sight of them, safe and whole.

"What's going on?" I asked, struggling free of Seradon and Marcus. I thought I knew the answer, but I didn't want to be right.

"That's the largest null pocket I've ever seen," Seradon said, confirming my fear.

"Damn!" Marcus stopped short, steadying Kylie when she tripped into him.

I stared at the nothingness around the marmot, fighting back a tide of helplessness. The agony of just my legs trapped in a null field had been overwhelming. When I'd foolishly submerged myself in the tiny pocket, I had felt like I was dying. Gargoyles lived and breathed magic. Existing without it wouldn't simply be agony; it'd kill the marmot. I didn't know how much time he had left, but it couldn't be long.

"We've got to get him out of there. How do we break it?"

"The same way I broke the one that trapped you," Marcus answered. "We have to push magic from the center outward to destabilize the field."

"We don't have much time," Grant said, taking the words from my mouth.

"It's expanding!" Kylie gasped and backpedaled from her close examination of the null's surface. Her wide eyes darted to Grant's. "That's not how a null field works. They dissipate."

"In a normal world, yes, but this park was overwhelmed with pure elements. When the destructive pentagram drained it, it pulled all the balanced energy into one spot, and they negated each other."

In a massive way. The gargoyle sat at the center of the

null field, too far inside for me to reach, but I had to try. Every second of delay could cost the marmot his life.

"Boost me," I ordered, glancing toward the gargoyles. Oliver, Lydia, and Quinn had joined their siblings, perching on nearby pillars. Magic from all five opened inside me, filling me with almost as much strength as I'd had in the link. I grabbed it all and stepped into the null sphere.

10

P ain crumpled me and momentum alone propelled my next slow step deeper into the null field. The air coalesced around my body, tight as molasses and equally hard to breathe. My bones sprouted needles of agony, all pushing outward through my skin as magic leeched from my body. I stretched cramping fingers toward the marmot, pushing all my gargoyle-enhanced magic toward it, willing it to live. The other hand I left flung behind me in the normal air, pulling in every scrap of magic I could hold.

When Marcus had freed me from the small null pocket, he'd been able to direct his magic across the empty sphere to puncture it, but I couldn't push the elements more than a few inches from my outstretched hand. No matter how much I strained, the magic oozed from me, the elements squiggling chaotically before dissipating into the dense air and its all-consuming nothingness.

I shuffled another constricted step, and pain slid up the arm behind me and closed over my fingertips. All magic vanished. It didn't snap in a backlash. It didn't trickle to a thin thread. It ceased to exist, leaving only pain, and I was still a yard from the gargoyle.

I gasped for air, my equilibrium lost in the saturation of agony. I stepped back, reaching for magic, and my fingers crunched against an invisible wall, bending backward, the sting indistinguishable from the stabbing pain invading my entire body.

A strong hand shot through the null field's shell and clamped onto my forearm. Magic, sweet and soft, pulsed into me, and the wall softened. Marcus yanked me free of the null. I fell against him, limp, and he hooked his hands under my armpits to prevent me from collapsing at his feet. Every joint in my body ached as if I'd been sick with the flu for a week, but I could feel magic again. It settled against my skin like a balm, and I could have happily rolled in the feeling if I could have figured out how to work my muscles.

"What were you thinking?" Marcus bellowed.

"He's going to die." My words were frustratingly breathy. I might have sounded stronger if I could have lifted my head from Marcus's chest. Even better if tears didn't thicken my throat. Hadn't the marmot been through enough already? Every second it took us to save him was a moment of endless pain for him. "We have to save him. Can't waste time."

"Well, there goes my plan," Grant said, sarcasm thick in his voice.

"Give her a break. She's a healer. You know how they're never right in the head," Seradon said.

"Some less so than others," Marcus growled.

Clutching my temples, I silently conceded that I'd been rash. Panic and guilt ate at me as I stared at the helpless marmot, but with the slowly ebbing pain forcing me to take a moment to think, I recognized the stupidity of my actions.

Not looking at anyone, I righted myself, only to grab for

Marcus's forearm when my left foot contacted the ground and the sharp pain stole my breath as if the granite spear had been driven anew through my sole. The null field had negated the field patch.

Gritting my teeth, I centered my balance on my right foot and finally managed to stand on my own. Marcus squinted at me, then let me go.

"We need to unbalance the null," Grant said. "Velasquez, the hottest fire you've got."

Marcus stepped away from me, and I swayed in place. Kylie darted forward to prop me up. She might have said something, but my whole being was focused on the squad's rescue efforts.

Blue-white flame shot from Marcus's hands, setting fire to a bushel of plants Marciano grew from a crack in the marble. Grant snapped branches thicker than his legs from the downed sycamores, and he and Winnigan used bands of air to pile them atop Marcus's fire. Kylie directed a whirlwind of air through the surrounding area, collecting twigs and smaller branches to add to the flames. In less than a minute, the squad had built an unnaturally hot bonfire twice as tall as Marciano. Kylie helped me hobble backward away from the intense heat of the blue flames. Elemental fire magic flowed from the blaze, and it licked against the null field.

I held my breath, waiting for the first signs that the null was shrinking. Against the building power of the singular element, it should have destabilized.

The null crept across the burning logs, smothering the roaring fire to soft orange flickers. No elemental magic formed around the flames inside the null. Fire without the element? How was that even possible?

"So much for that plan," Marcus said, dampening the

fire to coals. Elemental strands shifted above the embers to twine up the outside edge of the null sphere.

"Are you up for linking yet?" Grant asked Seradon.

She shook her head. "Still can't lift a pebble."

"Okay. Mika, sit your ass down before you fall down and link up. We're forming a bridge and getting to the heart of this."

I didn't wait until I was sitting; I thrust an equalized bundle of elements at Grant, and he deftly caught it, pulling me into a link. His thundercloud of magical strength swamped my thoughts; then Marcus's heated rosewood shield snapped into the link, followed by the cool slap of Winnigan's magic and a snarl of smoldering ironwood that must have been Marciano. Practice made it easier to distinguish each elemental in the link, but I didn't take any pleasure in the new skill since it got me no closer to saving the marmot.

I lowered myself to sit on a blob of marble. At one point, it'd probably been a bench, but the polarization had reshaped it into a black-veined lump of rock. Kylie kept a hand on my arm as if she thought I'd tip off the seat. When the gargoyles dropped into the link, opening a seemingly bottomless well of magic, I thought Kylie's concern might be justified. Magic roared through me, and I teetered on the edge of control. Losing myself in the magic was tempting. If I let go and lost myself, I'd be buffered from my pain.

I'd also be useless to the marmot.

I am a gargoyle healer. I didn't really need the words to collect myself this time, but it helped me to hear it, even if it was only in my thoughts.

"Are you okay?" Kylie asked. "Can I do anything?"

I shook my head. At one time, I would have thought this

amount of magic could solve any problem. Now I knew better. All magic had its limits.

Grant and Marcus clasped forearms, and Marciano grabbed hold of Marcus's other arm. Winnigan trotted to my side and reached for me. She stood close enough for us to lock arms without me needing to stand; then she and Marciano linked up so we made a human chain. Seradon stood back out of the way, her face a mask of frustration. Not being able to help must have been tearing her up inside.

I glanced at the marmot. I knew exactly how she felt.

The captain eased into the null field, arms splayed, one toward the gargoyle, the other toward Marcus. Tight lines formed around his eyes and his face whitened, but if I hadn't been inside the null myself, I never would have known pain ate through his body from the inside out.

Grant drew on all our magic, and I swayed toward him. I wasn't the only one; the squad tilted toward the captain as the forcible suction of the elements through us tilted our equilibrium.

Grant funneled all the magic out of the palm he stretched toward the marmot. The captain's long arms enabled him to progress a few feet closer to the marmot than I had, but despite the massive level of our combined power, little more magic escaped into the null. With another step, his fingers on Marcus's arm slid past the invisible barrier, submerging Grant in the null field.

The link frayed and magic whiplashed. With a cry, I cut myself free of the wild energy, and an explosion of raw elements burst into the air. A backdraft of wind pressed me to the marble and knocked Kylie to her butt; then it dissipated. Down the line, elements bloomed from the squad, displacing the air with audible snaps and pops. Inside the bubble, the captain stood several feet from the center, not even close enough to touch the marmot.

"Grant!" Kylie picked herself up and darted toward the null field. Seradon intercepted her.

The captain turned, his body hunched, and reached for Marcus, having lost contact in the wild release of magic. Marcus and Marciano both reached into the field, feeding their individual magic into Grant and yanking him free.

The marmot remained imprisoned in the middle of the null, as helpless to free himself as we were to reach him.

"It's not dissipating or weakening," Winnigan said, massaging her temples. "It's *eating* magic and getting stronger."

Chills tingled down my spine. Elsa had a lot to answer for. Her attempt to manufacture her own gargoyle-like enhancement had backfired in the worst way possible—and after having experienced the polarized magic, that was saying something.

"How big could the null field get?" Kylie asked.

I caught the anxious look Winnigan and Grant shared, and fresh dread weighted my stomach. If they were worried, I should be paralyzed with fear.

"It might stop where the polarization stopped," Winnigan said. "It might not. We've never dealt with anything like this."

If the null field got that big, the marmot would certainly die. The fox, too. If it didn't stop expanding, all magic would cease to exist and everyone would die. We *had* to get magic to the center. But how? I looked around, desperately hoping a solution would drop out of the air.

"A bridge," Marciano said. He was a man of few words, and he didn't waste any now.

Grant snapped his fingers and pointed at Marciano.

"Right. If we can't be the bridge, we can make one. Something physical. With one of us on the inside guiding the magic, this could work."

"Here." Marciano wrapped wood, fire, and water around the branch of one of the remaining standing sycamores. The limb came free and Marciano's magic stitched the bark together to repair the damage. Even as the limb floated toward us on hefty bands of air, Marciano reshaped it, stretching and growing the branch until it was thinner than my wrist and long enough to span the null field.

"Good," Grant said, plucking the pole from the air.

"It won't work," I said. I'd caught sight of my pack, tossed aside when I arrived and forgotten in what had become the water section when we fled.

I shoved from my marble seat before my doubts could catch up with the impractical hope surging through me. I hopped across the uneven ground and dropped beside the waterlogged bag. Cold mud squished under my knees and soaked through my pants as I fumbled with the drawstring on the bag. When it wouldn't loosen, I snapped it with a sharp twist of earth.

"Mika?" Marcus asked.

"Explain yourself, Healer," Grant demanded.

I yanked Kylie's soggy library books and my ruined notebook from the bag and flung them out of the way, then upended the bag. Clear seed crystals poured into the mud, all twenty-five pounds scattering in front of me.

"Wood is weak," I said. "It's too malleable and the grain in the wood will fracture our magic. You and I both had a hard enough time pushing magic from our bodies; we'd have to work five times as hard to funnel it through a branch. Quartz accepts all elements better. It'll be a stronger, cleaner bridge."

I'd worked with seed crystals a thousand times, a hundred thousand times; effortlessly, I wrapped them in quartz-tuned earth magic and fused them together. When Oliver, then the other gargoyles, dropped magic into me, the crystals flew through the air too fast for my eyes to track, but I didn't need to see what I was doing. I ran feelers of earth across the ground, and every crystal sang to me. I could differentiate the subtle variations in each one and discern how they'd best align together without looking. Even unaided, I could have mustered enough air to lift the crystals into place, but with the help of the gargoyles, the marble-size seeds were as light as grains of sand. The bar grew in a seamless length, complete before I finished talking.

"True," Seradon said. She paused to take in the finished rod. "But you're not the strongest elemental. It should be Marciano inside the null guiding the magic."

"No. I'm the gargoyle healer. I'm going in." I stood, lifting the quartz pole like a staff. It towered over me.

"This is about more than saving the gargoyle," Marcus said.

"Of course. This is about saving magic itself, which includes saving all magic creatures, gargoyles included." *But especially this marmot.* If the null continued to expand, a lot of lives were in jeopardy, but right now, only one was and I was the best person to help him. "Besides, none of you are stronger with quartz than me."

I sounded brave. I probably even looked brave since the quartz rod was helping me stand up straight. I was filthy, bloody, and battered, and I wasn't backing down.

I did my best not to acknowledge how terrified I was. This could go wrong in so many ways that if I didn't keep moving, I'd be paralyzed with doubt. I was counting on my quartz specialty to be enough, but it might not be. And if it wasn't, I could be dooming the marmot gargoyle. I could be dooming everyone. The more times we failed to break the null and the longer it existed, the stronger and bigger it grew. If I failed, it might be too big to stop the next time, even by a stronger elemental. Plus, there was the crushing pain of the null itself and the very real possibility I'd run out of air before I even reached the center.

But I wouldn't back down. Not only had I proven myself capable of doing things today that even these elite FPD warriors didn't know were possible, but also *I was a gargoyle healer.* I was supposed to protect the gargoyles in this city, yet I'd been oblivious to the marmot's needs and he'd been trapped and tortured on my watch. I wasn't going to fail him again.

"Break the quartz into five pieces," Marcus said.

Grant nodded. He turned to Kylie. "Reporter, it's time to do something useful for once."

While I severed the quartz rod into five pieces and gently coaxed them all to the length of the original piece, Winnigan accepted a bundle of elements from Kylie. My best friend would be the fifth person in their link, taking my place on the outside.

Seradon examined the slender rods. Quartz might be one of the strongest rocks in the world, but anything stretched too thin became fragile, and the five rods were now hardly thicker than my pinkie finger. They'd snap if I stepped on them, but they could still support their own weight, so they would have to be strong enough.

"You'll need to use all the magic together, and you won't have a lot of energy left to combine it manually once you're in the null," Seradon said. "If you fuse the bridges together, it'll give you one place to hold and allow the magic to mingle."

"Good thinking." With Seradon's help, I arranged the rods on the ground so the ends made five perfect wedges and the tips formed an apple-size pentagon at the center. A few twists of quartz element and they were fused.

"I never would have called you into this mess if I'd known it was going to be this dangerous," Seradon said.

Surprised, I looked up into her worried brown eyes.

"It should be me going into the null," she said.

"Aww, FPD guilt. That's cute."

Seradon's laugh came out as a bark, and she clapped me on the back.

A rumble of earth shook the plateau as Grant guided the magic of the link into the sinkhole, lifting a slab of mud-covered hornfels to replace the missing chunk of ground. When he finished, the group circled my lines of quartz, each standing at an end. Seradon moved out of the way, a serious expression replacing her momentary mirth. A glow of magic surrounded me, swirling in the link between the others. I shared a glance with Kylie, reading my own fears in her large blue eyes. She managed a tremulous smile, and I tried to return it.

Everyone picked up a rod and I lifted the central pentagon. Together we walked toward the null.

"Kylie, let go and circle around," Grant ordered. Her rod needed to pass through the null and out the other side before she could grab it again. The rest of the rods were long enough for the squad to hang on to the tips without encountering the expanding null sphere.

I slid my hand down the slender quartz as Kylie let it go, lifting the fragile bridge higher so the sagging tip didn't catch on the ground and snap. Kylie darted around the null to take her place on the other side, and the squad and I shifted to align the spokes to avoid hitting the marmot.

Taking a deep breath, I released all magic and stepped into the null.

———

NOTHINGNESS PUNCHED ME IN THE GUT AND THE PAIN blossomed in all directions through my body. I fought against panic, striving for even breaths. My lungs pumped dense air, starving on the too-thin oxygen. No matter how deeply I inhaled, I couldn't quite catch my breath.

Leaning into the soupy null field, I locked eyes on the marmot and focused on moving my feet one agonizing step at a time. My heart constricted at the sight of him. No longer blinded by panic and without the film of elements that coated the outer layer of the null sphere muddying the view, I beheld the toll today's numerous traumas had inflicted on the gargoyle. All color had leeched from his former earthy brown and blue-tipped body; he looked like a statue carved from a chunk of slate and as equally devoid of life.

Hang on. I'm coming.

The null drank magic from me, siphoning it from my muscles and knotting my joints until I hobbled on cramped feet and bowed legs. In the oddly thick environment, increasing my pace proved as impossible as jogging at the bottom of a lake. No energy lifted from the earth; no element twined through the air currents. The physical pieces were all in place, but without magic, the world felt dead. Even sounds were muffled and indistinct.

My hand spasmed on the delicate quartz pentagon, and it flexed in my grip. My fingers curled, the pain gnarling them into a fist against my will. I stopped on quivering legs and let go of the unsupported pole to use my free hand to pry my gnarled fingers from the pentagon. If I crushed it, I'd have to start all over, wasting time the marmot didn't have.

I almost dropped the pentagon as I maneuvered the two rods I stood between to rest on my shoulders, with the pentagon pressing against my throat. Afraid to hold the unsupported quartz pole in my cramping hand and risk snapping it, I used the back of my hand to lift the sagging tip. The slender quartz weighed no more than five pounds, but it felt like fifty.

My feet had taken root. I strained forward, pushing into the excruciating molasses, and heaved the lead weight of my throbbing foot. I kept my eyes pinned on the marmot, my entire existence narrowing to reaching him. Five minutes or five hours later, the fingers of my free hand brushed against his cold chest. The weight of Kylie's quartz line lifted and I stumbled the last two steps on what felt like the broken bones of my own feet.

The marmot appeared no better up close. No life pulsed beneath my hand. Even though I'd told myself I wouldn't be able to feel anything without magic, it still came as a shock. He felt like a piece of carved rock.

Please don't be dead. Please don't be dead.

I leaned close to the gargoyle, until the V of the two quartz rods cut into my neck and two separate lines rested against the marmot's slender shoulders. He was the center of everything, and short of climbing him, this was the closest I could get to the heart of the null.

Very carefully, I closed my fingers around the pentagon. Magic trickled into me, soothing the persistent burn of the null in my fingertips. For a second, the relief swelled through me; then the misery of the other ninety-nine percent of my body overwhelmed my senses again.

I drew the magic to me—and gritted my teeth as the pain in my extremities increased in response. I could feel the others at the end of the quartz lines and the gargoyles inside their link. They held overwhelming magic, but no matter how they strained to shove it to me, the null strangled their copious magic to the merest trickle. It would be enough. It had to be.

I pushed every scrap of magic I could touch into the null. The soft lines of loose elements drifted in the vacuum and vanished a few inches from the quartz.

Black spots danced in my vision as my brain tried to shut down to protect itself from the pain, and I abandoned that tactic. I needed more magic than I could pull, and continuing to use the tiny trickle squeezing through the quartz wasn't going to cut it. In torturous increments, I refined the incoming magic into the five elements, layering them around the pentagram in the constructive cycle: earth, water, wood, air, fire. The magic in the rods shifted to align the incoming elemental energy to match my pentagon as the others caught on to what I was doing.

I planned on letting the constructive cycle do the work for me and build up its strength until it had enough magic to make an impact when I released it into the null, but it didn't increase, or if it did, it wasn't quick.

While I waited, my feet and legs went numb. The pain didn't abate, but I couldn't feel the muscles anymore. I couldn't find my foot to lift or my knee to bend. I couldn't move or escape. Panting, I sucked in volumes of empty null and very little oxygen. At this rate, I'd suffocate before the magic built up to a usable level in the pentagon. I needed to create a faster, stronger constructive cycle—the strongest I'd ever encountered.

I needed to use the purifier's constructive pattern.

Oh, the irony.

I'd spent the last hour countering the purifier's powerful helix braids. I knew them intimately. If I'd had a chance to think about it, I would have said I would take the knowledge of those destructive, horrific weaves to my grave, determined to never let them see the light of day again. Yet, less than a half hour later I was reconstructing them and praying it would save us.

Knowing what the weaves looked like and re-creating them with thimblefuls of magic were two very different concepts. To keep the trickle of magic flowing, the constructive pattern along the pentagon had to be maintained, so I was forced to build the helixes into the empty air at the center of the pentagon, unanchored. The elements kept slipping from my grasp and evaporating into the null. Every time I held two elements long enough to twine them together, fire ate through my body as the null tried to pull my skin inside out. The jabbing, pounding pain in my skull should have long since liquefied my brain. Part of me hoped it would. Soon. Just to make the pain stop.

Numbness crept up my hips and abdomen. I clung to the marmot with my free hand, afraid I'd topple. Three braids down and bands of steel nothingness tightened around my lower ribs, constricting my limited oxygen even further. The black dots were back, but this time I couldn't stop. Even if I did, it wouldn't help. The null had me in its jaws and it wasn't going to let me go.

I formed the final helix braid as the paralysis slid over my chest. I'd divided the inner space of the pentagon into five triangles, creating an inverted purifier with all the spokes pointing inward. With a final twist, I connected the free tips of the braids using a minuscule constructive loop, then released it.

Please be alive. I stared into the gargoyle's dead eyes, feeling the life suck from me. Air was a fond memory. *You'd better live. You'd better make this worth it.*

Magic swirled in the pentagon faster than before, but nothing happened. Not even tiny tendrils of magic released to counter the null. I'd failed.

I clung to the marmot, and his statue-like arms supported me under my armpits. My legs must have collapsed, because I was looking at the marmot's pock-marked chest instead of his eyes.

"Hold, damn it!" Grant's order penetrated the void, his voice muffled like it was filtered through a wall of rugs.

My neck went limp, and I remembered to loll my head back, away from the quartz pentagon. I couldn't crush the pentagon.

Kylie stood at the end of her quartz rod, and though her expression was intent, tears coursed down her cheeks. Marcus stood at the next quartz rod, his face beet red and veins at his temple protruding as he shouted over my head at Grant.

"... have to get her ... killing her ..."

Crap. I was dying. I mustered my energy and fought to remain conscious, to draw a breath, to live. The void smacked me down as easily as I might crush an ant. My will petered out.

11

D arkness closed around my irises, narrowing the world to a pinpoint. A compressed cyclone of elements shot from the pentagon in a flat disk, slicing along the bands of quartz. They hit the null's boundary and it imploded. Magic hit me with the slap of a belly flop against my entire body. The elements poured into me, igniting every fiber of my being in fiery agony.

Then air rushed into my lungs, and for a glorious instant, my body was absolutely pain-free. As if in slow motion, the purifier's braids multiplied and swelled along the quartz rods before blasting outward, mindlessly hunting for the nearest gargoyles in their paths.

I'd saved us only to doom us.

No. Not again.

Pain sank back into my body, but it was an echo of the previous crippling agony and unimportant. Yanking the pentagon over my head, I turned my back to the marmot to shield it and smashed the purifier-lined crystal rods against the marble. Shards of quartz exploded and magic ripped from the pieces, bursting apart and slamming me into the gargoyle. His hard paws jabbed my ribs and my head snapped back against the solid rock of his neck.

My brain rang like a struck gong between my ears. Magic unraveled inside me, eating along my neural pathways. My knees gave out and I crumpled to the shard-strewn marble. A pillow of air cradled my head before it hit the ground, and I fought to keep my eyes open. The marmot still needed me.

A rush of warmth cascaded from my scalp to my toes. Fire magic slid into my bones, accompanied by a peripheral feeling of rosewood and traces of lightning. Marcus. Tension uncoiled in my stomach; I was safe. Cool water and veins of wood spun around me, sinking slowly into my skin until they met up with the warmth of the fire in my bones, restoring the magic leeched from me and leaving me blissfully numb.

"It's just a field patch," Marcus said. His voice rumbled against my ear.

He held me cradled against his chest. I was too euphoric from the lack of pain to care that I looked like a complete wimp. I allowed myself exactly five breaths to savor the glorious lack of pain before I struggled to stand. Marcus assisted me, not commenting when I had to brace a hand on his shoulder to stay upright after he set me on my feet.

I reached for magic, and it trickled to me along scalded mental pathways. My legs almost gave out with relief. I hadn't nullified myself.

Oliver dropped from the pillar where he'd perched and landed next to me. He wrapped a wing around my leg, giving me much needed stability. Lydia swooped to land beside Marcus. She gently nipped at his shirt, then bumped his forearm with her rock head and leaned into him. Half grown, she came to his waist. She was going to be a huge gargoyle. The other siblings dropped to the ground and circled the marmot. Herbert flapped ungracefully when the muddy ground of the former water section suctioned to his armadillo paws, and he hopped a few feet to the left.

The five gargoyles opened their magical boost to me, but I didn't accept it. The pain behind what little magic I held told me not to push myself. It felt like I'd sprained my brain, and I needed to heal before I could work magic at full strength, let alone gargoyle-enhanced levels.

I didn't need the boost to form a soft probe, either. I slid the gargoyle-tuned mix of elements into the marmot, holding my breath. He'd been stabbed repeatedly, used as a magic pump, assaulted by polarized magic, and suffocated in a null. On top of that, he suffered from a disease that left him comatose. It was foolish to hope he'd survived.

His fragile life beat deep inside his jasper body. My breath shook when I released it. He teetered on the edge of life, fractured by magic and pain and the mysterious dormancy disease. Using the thinnest, most delicate bands of jasper-tuned earth and soft brushes of fire, I fed him magic. As I moved the elements through him, I wove gossamer-fine patches over his fractures and watched as his body absorbed my magic and used it to begin to heal. His frailty dictated my speed—achingly slow—and the extent to which I could assist him. Well before he was whole, I eased my magic from him. Anything more would overtax his system and do more damage than good.

I blinked at a world washed with muted pink and orange. It took my sluggish brain several seconds to connect the light with the sunset—longer to realize that I stared up at the sky because Marcus held me cradled in his arms.

Again.

How embarrassing.

"Will he live?" Marcus asked when I focused on his face.

"Yes. With more healing." With all the trauma he'd experienced, I hadn't been able to identify the cause of his coma, but that problem would have to wait until tomorrow. Or the next day. I needed to do some recovering of my own first.

"I think I can stand," I said. It felt silly for him to be holding me.

"Mmm." Marcus sat and placed me on the ground next to him. I decided it was a good compromise. "Grant has summoned healers."

"Oh, good." As wonderful as Marcus's field patches were at numbing the pain, I needed true healing. So did Seradon and Marcus.

In the fading sunlight, the devastated park looked like the aftermath of a horrific war between elementals. Winnigan and Marciano stood at the bottom of the plateau, facing Lincoln River. Winnigan had removed her shoes to stand with her toes in the receding pool, and soft bands of the element twined up her legs, absorbing into her skin. Marciano stood behind her, his arms wrapped around the much smaller woman, his chin resting on her head. Silently, they soaked in the sunset. I hadn't realized they were a couple, but somehow the giant and the petite redhead fit together.

Grant, Seradon, and Kylie sat at the end of a shattered line of quartz where Kylie had been standing when we broke the null. Her slumped posture indicated her exhaustion, but it didn't stop her from pestering them with questions.

"You'll recover faster if you don't talk," Grant advised.

Kylie visibly gathered herself to argue, but Seradon spoke first. "I think she's earned a few answers."

Grant scowled, then nodded. Kylie graced him with a

triumphant grin, and it made me smile. She couldn't have been hurt if she was still angling for her story. Or at least not *badly* hurt. She looked up and met my gaze, tossing me a wink Grant couldn't see.

"In that case," she said, "let's start at the beginning. You said a concerned citizen reported Elsa. How were you contacted? What was your first impression of the scene?"

Grant's grumpy one-word responses seemed to amuse Seradon. I had no doubt Kylie would coax the whole story from the captain, but I tuned them out. I didn't want to relive today, not now and especially not knowing that my own Kylie interrogation lurked in my future.

"Are you okay?" I asked Marcus.

One dark eyebrow lifted. "Why wouldn't I be?"

"Right, this was just another day in a full-five squad."

"Are you mad?"

I shook my head. I was, but it was petty. I felt like I'd been pressed through a mesh strainer and clumsily reassembled while he merely looked a little tired.

"I wasn't the one inside the null," he said, as if he could read my mind.

"What was it like on the outside?"

His gaze slid down my face to rest on my hand. At some point, Oliver had tucked his sinuous body against my side, and I absently stroked his wings where I'd healed them earlier. The rest of his body still needed attention. *Soon,* I promised us both silently.

The other gargoyles remained around the marmot, and their eyes drooped. I sent soft test weaves through them, reassuring myself that all my gargoyles were okay. The ordeal with the purifier and the null had exhausted them, but they'd recover.

"Like running in quicksand," Marcus said, finally

answering my question. "I had so much magic available to me, but no matter how hard I pushed it down the quartz, only a trickle reached you. It felt like I was doing nothing but watching you . . . watching you be drained." He paused, lifting his face toward the sunset. "Useless. Being on the outside felt useless."

I wasn't sure what to say. The sunset turned the high clouds from pink to purple. Nearby, a bird sang a lullaby to the sun and a few crickets added sharp accompaniment.

"The gargoyles were true heroes," he said. Oliver lifted his head, bright eyes shining in the twilight. "I've never encountered a null that big—not even half that big. Without their help, we wouldn't have been enough. As it is, it's going to be days before any of us can work magic at full capacity. Right now, without us linking back up, you're probably the strongest elemental in the park."

Huh. So he was human after all.

"You saved us twice today," I said to Oliver. "Terra Haven owes you a medal of honor."

Oliver hummed, a quiet, happy sound. Despite everything he'd been through, he was more balanced and healthy-looking internally than if he'd spent a week safely ensconced in my apartment. His siblings were listing on their feet, but he was alert.

"You have a warrior's spirit, Oliver," Marcus said.

He was right. I took a deep breath and acknowledged a truth I'd been hiding from myself: Oliver needed more than me. His siblings were all exploring roosting locations throughout the city, places they could call home where they felt a resonance with the inhabitants and environment. But Oliver had remained with me, and it wasn't simply because he liked me better than the others did. He wasn't like his siblings. He wasn't ready to settle into one place. He was more adventurous. He was happiest when we were rushing toward a gargoyle in need. He was a rare gargoyle who thrived on action.

I leaned around Marcus and called to Grant. We were close enough to converse, but he promptly extricated himself from Kylie's conversation and strode to my side. I didn't miss the way he glanced back at my best friend, though, and there was nothing grumpy about his expression. Maybe Kylie didn't bother him as much as he pretended.

"What can I do for you, gargoyle healer?"

"Could you use a gargoyle in your unit?"

Grant's eyes widened and his eyebrows flicked up. "Is there a willing gargoyle?"

I glanced at Oliver. The young gargoyle watched me curiously.

"You'll never find a better group of people to work with, Oliver," I said, my heart breaking. Oliver had been a true hero today, and he'd thrived in the role. I'd been selfish to keep him as my companion. It was time to set him free. "You're courageous and strong—a real warrior, like Marcus said. I don't think you'll ever be happy in just one place. You need adventure."

"We have adventures," Oliver said, his brow furrowed.

"Sure, every once in a while. But the squad has experiences like this every day."

"You were a real asset today," Grant said. "I'd be honored to have you on my team."

Oliver perked up.

"Think of all the important work you could do with them. You could save Terra Haven every day." I wouldn't cry. This was for the best. With the squad, Oliver could do what he loved, and the squad would keep him safe and healthy.

He'd be happy. "I think you'd make a great addition to Captain Monaghan's squad."

"Really, Mika? Do you think so?" Oliver's tiny ears quivered behind his carnelian ruff.

"I do. This is your calling, Oliver." A bittersweet ache settled in my chest, partially assuaged by knowing I was putting his well-being above my own needs. This was how a true gargoyle healer behaved.

Oliver leapt to his feet with an excited trill that echoed through the park, and the pressure in my chest eased. This was the right call. I swallowed the lump in my throat, and forced a smile that turned genuine when Oliver launched straight into the air, shouting, "I am a *warrior*!"

12

I limped down the library steps and turned to wait for Oliver to glide down to meet me. Pigeons cooed and bobbed along the roofline, but the blue sky remained empty. I turned away, my heart constricting with familiar soreness. It'd been almost two weeks since Oliver had departed with the FPD, and I'd thought it'd be easier by now. For the twentieth time today, I assured myself that I'd made the right decision in encouraging him to go with the squad. Remembering his excitement helped.

Distractions worked better.

I purchased a copy of the *Terra Haven Chronicle* from a newsboy on the corner and hobbled to lean against the brick wall of a building, out of the way of traffic. The healers had done a wonderful job mending my foot, though it'd hurt worse than the original injury. I had another week of wearing a brace while the freshly knitted tissue and muscle strengthened before I'd be cleared to walk unimpeded. I was counting the hours.

The front page of the paper focused on the recent governor's debate and had nothing to do with me, gargoyles, the full-five squad, or Focal Park. I breathed a sigh of relief. I'd had the dubious honor of gracing the front page again, thanks to Kylie. Sometime before the healers had arrived, she'd snapped a picture of me, Marcus, and the marmot behind us. I'd looked like a disaster victim, not a hero, especially next to Marcus, who even in repose managed to appear ready to rush off to halt a swarming clutch of basilisks. The headline had been equally embarrassing: *Gargoyle Healer Saves Terra Haven.* Kylie had a gift for writing, but she tended to exaggerate my heroism. Thankfully column space had been limited, and after she'd described everything else that had transpired thanks to Elsa's purifier, she'd only had two inches left to recount my destruction of the null. She still managed to make me seem impressive enough to be a member of the FPD.

I found Kylie's follow-up story on page 11 today. It detailed the ongoing cleanup at the park and a few facts about Elsa's career, ending with a simple statement: *Elsa Lansing remains under guard at the Soothing Halls mental hospital, awaiting trial.*

I folded the paper and stuffed it in my bag with my haul of books. I slung it over my shoulder and checked to see if Oliver was—

Releasing a sigh, I limped along the sidewalk and tried to picture a punishment a jury could dole out that would be worse than Elsa's current fate. In her greedy pursuit of more power, she had nullified herself. For the rest of her life, she'd be able to see magic but never touch or use it again.

I shuddered. The few minutes I'd spent inside the null field had been some of the most horrific of my life, even discounting the agony of having magic sucked through my skin from my bone marrow. Cut off from magic, the world had felt dead. I had felt dead. It would be a horrible existence.

Pausing, I searched for sympathy for Elsa, finding none. The dull headache that had been my constant companion since destroying the purifier thumped behind my temples. Drawing magic still hurt, especially in large quantities. The healer had assured me I would make a full recovery, but it would take longer than my foot.

If it had been just me Elsa had hurt, I might have been able to forgive her, but I couldn't forgive what she'd done to the gargoyles.

The day after my adventures in the park, I'd hunted down the four gargoyles in the city who had been trapped in the purifier's braids. Healing them had been simple enough for my overtaxed body and brain to handle; distance had weakened the purifier and limited the internal damage it inflicted. The marmot and fox hadn't been so lucky.

I caught sight of my grim expression in the reflection of a storefront window. My eyes looked harder than I remembered.

Turning away, I resumed my trek back to my apartment. I'd already visited the fox and marmot today. Focal Park remained closed to the general public while it was restored, but I was a gargoyle healer and had received a special guard detail to escort me in and out each day. With daily healing, both the fox and marmot had stabilized even though they remained unresponsive and paralyzed.

I wasn't giving up. I'd worked alongside a full-five squad to destroy an acres-wide mutation of magic. I'd split my spirit among my five gargoyles to save them from the purifier. I'd rescued the marmot from the largest null field anyone had ever seen. If I could do all that, I could solve the mystery of the dormancy disease and heal these gargoyles, too.

My extensive testing and probing in the marmot and fox hadn't revealed the source of the disease, so I'd turned to the library. If I couldn't find the problem within the gargoyles, maybe I could find answers in the manuals of previous healers and in scholarly journals. I'd checked out every book, newspaper, and scroll that even hinted at a dormancy sickness, and when I'd tapped out the resources of Terra Haven's library, I'd special ordered material from around the country.

Between recuperating, doctoring the fox and marmot, administering to more mundane gargoyle sicknesses, and doing research, I had almost managed to keep myself busy enough to not miss Oliver.

When Ms. Zubberie's Victorian came into sight, I sighed with relief. My awkward hobble was tiring and the books in my bag were heavy. I was looking forward to getting upstairs to the room I rented and flopping onto the bed for the rest of the day.

An enormous orange rock plummeted from the roof, unfurling its wings a few feet above the ground. Oliver hit the ground running, using his wings to augment his short legs.

"Oliver!" My heart performed an acrobatic performance in my chest, soaring with elation and dipping back behind protective walls. I couldn't read too much into this. He was probably just visiting or needed a checkup.

I dropped my bag and crouched in time to brace myself. Oliver skidded to a halt in front of me and wrapped me in his massive eagle wings. It was like being hugged by a flexible wall, one that snuffled my hair and made soft crooning sounds of happiness. I hugged him back, patting his cool sides. Life and magic practically burst from him, and though I knew it was only a figment of my imagination, he seemed like he'd grown an extra foot since I'd last seen him.

"I'm so glad you came to visit," I said when he released me, sitting so close to me he was almost on top of me. I shifted my weight to my knees, shocked to notice that even with his stubby legs we were almost eye to eye.

"This isn't a visit," he said.

"It's not?" My heart plummeted. Did he need my help? He looked healthy. I'd healed the bulk of his raw patches before sending him off to his new home, and the intervening time had smoothed out the rest. If I was being honest, he looked better than healthy; he glowed. Life with the squad had been far better for Oliver than life with me, and the realization was a fresh jab to a raw wound.

Marcus stepped from the shadows of the Victorian's balcony. My breath hitched at the sight of him, and I told myself it was because he'd surprised me. He wasn't in uniform, but even in civilian clothing, no one would mistake him for anything other than an FPD man. From his impressive frame straining the seams of his off-white shirt to the graceful way he moved, everything about him spoke of years of training.

He trotted down the front steps, and I searched his expression. Some of my alarm died at the sight of the barely there smile softening the hard planes of his face, but I rose to my feet anyway. I hadn't forgotten how big Marcus was, and I didn't want to be towered over, especially since even once I was standing his height enabled him to pull off some impressive looming. Plus, the last time he'd seen me, I'd been limp from exhaustion and injuries. I wanted to emphasize my strength and recovery. See, the little gargoyle healer can handle herself.

I wanted to impress him. Oh, crap, I had a crush on the growly fire elemental.

"What's wrong?" I asked, hoping my voice sounded normal.

"Nothing. Oliver just wanted to come home. He says his place is here, with you."

I stilled, holding in selfish hope.

Oliver stared up at me with adoration. "I need to help you," he said.

"But what about the excitement and adventure?"

"Life with you is more exciting."

"Maybe the squad had an off couple of weeks." I glanced to Marcus and he shook his head.

"We rounded up a litter of unchained kludde pups invading the blight. It was pretty dicey stuff."

"And I met a manticore," Oliver added.

"You did?" How could life with me compete with that?

"It was fun, but our work is more important," Oliver said.

"'Our work'?" I echoed.

"Protecting gargoyles."

I blinked. Is that how he saw what I did? "With the squad, you have endless magic to feed on. Look at you; you're glowing with good health."

"That's pure coming-home glow," Marcus said. Oliver's tongue lolled out of his mouth and flapped when he nodded vigorously.

"Are you sure, Oliver?"

"Yes. I promise I'll make sure I balance my magic. You won't have to worry about me. Unless . . ." His wings wilted against his body. "Unless you don't want me."

The barrier around my hope shattered, melting my body's stiffness. I'd been so determined to make sure Oliver had a life he loved and a place to call home, I'd failed to see he'd already found it. With me.

"I'd be the luckiest person in all of Terra Haven to have you, Oliver." I blinked back happy tears and knew my grin looked almost as goofy as the gargoyle's.

"Oliver knows where we live. He's welcome to come by anytime," Marcus said.

I ran my fingers across the gargoyle's glossy forehead, and he closed his eyes in bliss, leaning into my leg. Marcus grabbed my arm when I staggered under Oliver's weight. I glanced up, and the warmth in his lapis lazuli eyes stole my breath.

"You're welcome anytime, too," he added.

He stepped back and flashed me his thousand-dollar smile. I closed my mouth with a click.

"You know, Oliver's not the only one with a warrior's spirit. Have you ever considered training to be in the FPD?"

"Me?" Surely he was joking.

"You proved you can think under pressure. You'd be an asset to a team."

I tried to picture myself working alongside Marcus, dealing with rampaging kludde and malfunctioning magic on a daily basis. I shook my head. "I'm flattered but no. I've found my place in life. Healing gargoyles is more than enough for me."

Marcus nodded. "I thought as much. But if you ever change your mind or you're ever in my neighborhood, drop by." He clapped me on the shoulder and said farewell to Oliver. I was pretty sure he also winked at me.

I pivoted to watch him walk away, blushing to my roots when he glanced back and caught me staring.

"Did you miss me?" Oliver asked.

"Every single second. Come on, let's go home."

Oliver fell in step beside me, and the imbalance inside me righted.

"Have you figured out what's wrong with the dormant gargoyles?" he asked.

"Not yet. But we will."

We climbed the steps of the Victorian side by side, as we'd done dozens of times before, but this time was special. My gargoyle was home to stay.

What's next for Mika and the gargoyles?

_____

Read on for a sneak peek from
REBECCA CHASTAIN'S
next Gargoyle Guardian Chronicles novel.

_____

AVAILABLE NOW!

SECRET OF THE GARGOYLES
GARGOYLE GUARDIAN CHRONICLES BOOK 3

I fanned a tiny hummingbird feather back and forth, collecting the swirling air element from the breeze before scooping up the soft bands of fire element from a guttering candle flame. An equal mix of water element came from a bowl of spring water, and wood element from a pot of wheatgrass. Splitting my concentration, I kept the four-element cocktail spinning to one side and plucked a quartz seed crystal from my pocket.

I tuned a tendril of earth magic to quartz and used it to flatten and stretch the marble-size crystal. When the tensile structure of the quartz began to give, threatening to crack, I eased my magic out of the crystal. The flattened disk lay across my right palm, barely a foot and a half across and so thin it bent toward the ground around the edges. Hopefully it'd be enough.

"Stand back, Oliver," I said, glancing toward my gargoyle companion.

He undulated sideways, his carnelian Chinese dragon body moving as fluidly as a flesh-and-blood dragon's.

"Is this good, Mika?" he asked, studying the motionless sick gargoyle in front of me. Oliver didn't voice the doubts I read in his glowing sunset-orange eyes, and his magic boost never wavered. He wanted this to work as badly as I did.

"Yep. Here it goes."

The sick gargoyle's marmot body had once been a beautiful brown jasper, with vivid blue dumortierite tipping his reindeer antlers and long wings, but now he was pockmarked and only a few dull shades more colorful than gray. From his lifeless brown eyes to his rigid posture, everything about the marmot gargoyle looked dead, but he was only dormant. Inside him, a spark of life remained, and I was determined to wake him from his comatose state.

Ignoring the chilly morning air that brushed my stomach when I raised my arms, I lifted the sheet of quartz high above the gargoyle. Standing on his hind legs, the marmot was almost eye level with me, and his antlers cleared my head by several feet. Ideally, I would have placed the thin quartz across his antlers, but their points were too far apart, so I settled for positioning the quartz above his head. With exaggerated care, I layered the four-element mix across the surface of the quartz disk, gradually sinking it into the thin membrane until the clear crystal swirled with magic. Hardly breathing, I collected air to cushion the bottom of the quartz, then retracted my hand. The disk remained floating above the marmot.

Crossing my fingers, I backed up, buried my eyes in the crook of my elbow, and dropped the quartz onto the marmot. The fragile sheet shattered, tiny grains spraying against my thighs. I lowered my arm. The five elements rolled down the marmot, coating his crown and ears, then muzzle, neck, wings, and stomach before sliding off his bottom toes and the tips of his stone feathers. The moment it touched the ground, the spell dissipated.

A fine glitter of quartz dust circled the marmot, and it crunched under my feet when I stepped closer to examine him. The gargoyle's eyes remained dull. His ears didn't twitch. Weaving a basic five-element pentagram, I tuned it to the gargoyle's resonance and tested him. His life pulsed against my magic, the reedy sensation encased in muted pain.

"No change." I brushed quartz dust from the marmot's upraised paws, then blew more from his forehead with a heavy sigh. It'd been silly to get my hopes up.

Many people believed gargoyles went through a dormant phase as a normal part of their lives, opting to check out for decades at a time, but my healer instincts said otherwise, and one test of the marmot's failing health had backed up my suspicion. Gargoyles typically enjoyed a sedentary life, choosing to remain near specific buildings for most of their days, but they still moved. Frequently. They were also picky about whose magic they enhanced, yet this paralyzed marmot gave a magic boost to anyone in the vicinity, as if his powers were as out of his control as his limbs. He was trapped inside his own body—and he wasn't the only one. I'd found six other dormant gargoyles in Terra Haven stuck in an identical dormant state.

"What now?" Oliver asked.

"We try something else," I said, which was better than saying, *I don't know.*

I slumped, dropping my forehead to rest against the marmot's. I'd already tried everything I could think of. I'd attempted healing him with and without Oliver's enhancement, beneath new and full moons and all the days in between, using exotic, expensive resources and basic seed crystals. I was running out of ideas—even the desperate ones, like today's modified, outdated spell originally designed to heal lethargy in humans—and the marmot was running out of time. Never strong to begin with, his life signs grew fainter every day. Even the other dormant gargoyles fared better than he did, but not by much.

Familiar weariness pulled my eyes closed. In the three months since I'd first learned about the comatose gargoyles, I'd been searching for a cure nonstop, and sleepless nights bent over my table scouring increasingly obscure references combined with a series of hope-crushing failures had sapped my energy.

"We'll find something, Mika." Oliver planted a paw on my hip, nuzzling my side, and I staggered beneath his weight.

"I know. Together we can do anything." The words tasted bitter.

A shouted curse pulled my head up, reminding me we weren't alone in Focal Park. A few hundred feet away, one of the cleanup crew tumbled into an enormous sinkhole, only to swing back up to solid ground on thick bands of air wielded by her four coworkers. She clutched the arm of the woman who grabbed her while one of the men reinforced the crumbling cliff, using hefty bands of earth element to reshape the granite beneath the topsoil and strengthen their footing.

The eroded crater in the middle of Terra Haven's premier park hadn't occurred naturally. Neither had the mutations in the botanical gardens or the flow of now-cool magma that had decimated a fifth of the grounds. The entire park had been deformed, all thanks to Elsa Lansing.

May she rot in prison.

Elsa had attempted to manually re-create a gargoyle's magical enhancement in an inanimate invention and failed spectacularly, nearly destroying the city along with Focal Park. But that was the least of her sins.

I ran a finger over five smooth patches on the marmot's neck. The clear crystal integrated into his fading brown jasper neck was my healer handiwork, and it'd taken me over a month to coax his weak body to graft enough layers of quartz to seal the five stab wounds. It turned out that to mimic a gargoyle's enhancement, Elsa had required the magic of a gargoyle, and she'd had no compunction against drilling into the marmot and draining his life to fuel her invention. Comatose and paralyzed, the marmot hadn't been able to fight back or even flee.

Rotting in prison was too good for Elsa, and knowing her invention had nullified her, leaving her unable to ever touch the elements again, was only a small consolation.

The earth rumbled behind me where towers of three-foot-wide granite pillars jutted from what had been a smooth slope before Elsa's invention went haywire. One of the taller granite posts snapped off at the base, then flew across the park to hover above the sunken ground. Cables of wood element pulverized the rock, crumbling the entire thousand-pound column into the gaping earth. Magic glowed around all five workers, funneling through the woman who had fallen into the pit, as they selected another pillar to demolish.

If not for my status as Terra Haven's sole gargoyle healer, I would have been banned from the hazardous park with the rest of the city's citizens during the restoration process. Instead, I had special clearance to tend to the marmot and one other dormant gargoyle in the park. The other, a large fox, lay out of the way atop a high granite outcrop, but after righting her internal imbalance caused by the invention's malicious magic, I'd stuck to the more accessible marmot for my healing experiments. He'd had the good sense to be on level ground when sickness struck, not perched at a vertigo-inducing height.

"Let's get this cleaned up, then see if the library has received the journal we special ordered," I said, unable to infuse any enthusiasm into my words.

"She's here," Oliver whispered.

My shoulders stiffened. I didn't need to turn to know he meant the onyx and amethyst gryphon gargoyle. She'd been following me around for the last month, observing from a distance any time I interacted with a dormant gargoyle—a critical witness to my repeated failures.

The first time she'd shown up, I'd thought she had come to help. Every gargoyle I'd asked about the dormancy sickness had refused to talk to me about it except for Oliver and his siblings, and they were as perplexed as I was—by the disease and by the other gargoyles' silence. But the gryphon was different. She'd helped me in the past: When Oliver had been a baby, he and his siblings had been kidnapped and imprisoned by Walter, a mercenary earth elemental who had tortured them to steal their magic for himself—and for the highest bidders in his black market scheme. While I'd been desperately trying to rescue the hatchlings, the gryphon had convinced the city guards to investigate my wild tale. Without her timely arrival, I wouldn't be alive, and neither would Oliver or his siblings.

I'd been wrong about her intentions now, though. The gryphon refused to let me or Oliver get close enough to talk, and I'd grown to resent her judgmental presence. It was bad enough that I hadn't found a cure after months of research and experimentation; having an audience made it ten times worse.

I ground my teeth and used a soft push of air to sweep the quartz powder into a pile. With Oliver's help, I packed up my supplies, the weight of the gryphon's censure boring into my back the entire time. Irritation made my movements clumsy. I didn't need the gryphon to point out my deplorable incompetence; I lived it every day, watching the dormant gargoyles slowly fade while I tried useless spells. My frustration with today's failure was made worse by the fact that I'd never really expected the spell to work; I simply hadn't had anything better to try—and I hadn't for weeks. But the gryphon's silent condemnation was the final straw.

"I've had enough of this." I spun and locked gazes with the gryphon. She lurked closer than normal, and I could easily make out her glowing lavender eyes, despite her location in the dappled shadows fifty yards away.

"Do you need help?" I called, my tone conveying the *butt out* meaning of my words. I projected my voice through a cone of air to direct it toward the gryphon and away from the cleanup crew. I didn't need them sticking their noses into this, too.

The gryphon's neck feathers ruffled, and sunlight ghosted across the ripple of onyx. Her hard eyes remained expressionless.

"Look, I'm doing my best here." I shrugged off Oliver's placating gesture and stomped up the incline toward the gryphon. "I'm trying everything I can think of, so unless you have any suggestions—"

The gryphon surged forward, leaping into the air on stone eagle wings and hurtling straight for me. I dropped to all fours to avoid being clipped by her massive eagle talons, my heart lifting into my throat. The backdraft of her wings whipped my hair into my eyes as she shot past us. She banked, spinning through the air as if she'd anchored one wingtip in the ether, and swooped back toward us. Her enormous body temporarily blocked the sun before she landed on silent stone feet close enough to snap my head off. Oliver reared up protectively in front of me, but even with his wings flared, his slender body looked fragile next to the gryphon. She ignored him, folding her enormous amethyst-striated onyx wings against her body and glaring at me.

"Stop shouting." The gryphon's voice was that of a lion's, soft and rumbling, despite forming in a rock throat and emerging through an eagle's beak.

"Uh, of course." I straightened on shaky legs and squared my shoulders.

Dismissing me and Oliver, she stalked around us to stare into the marmot's blank eyes. I released a quiet breath and patted Oliver. He dropped to all fours, keeping his wings partially cupped to give himself extra bulk. I shuffled in a wide arc around the gryphon until I could see her face again, and Oliver twined beside me, moving slower than normal. I think it was his version of being tough, and I appreciated the effort.

"I've been watching you," she said.

"I know—"

She turned the full weight of her stare on me, and my mouth clicked shut.

"I have talked with the gargoyles you've healed," she continued, "and I have talked with the gargoyles this cub has been spreading tales to."

Oliver bristled, the orange-red ruff around his face flaring. I crossed my arms. Was this where she accused me of being an unfit healer? If so, she was wrong. I'd been an exemplary healer—at least until I'd encountered the comatose gargoyles. She was welcome to point me in the direction of a more practiced healer or even a book that might provide an answer to the dormancy sickness, but otherwise I wasn't in the mood to listen to her recriminations.

"You risked much to save the hatchlings when they were so foolishly caught. You risked more to save Rourke."

My indignation faltered. She knew the sick gargoyle's name.

"I'm still trying to save him—to save Rourke," I said. "But you know that. You've watched me every day."

The gryphon acted as if I hadn't spoken, observing without speaking as the cleanup crew broke off another pillar of granite, spun it through the air, and crumbled it into the deep pit on the other side of the park.

I tried to read her expression. She didn't look ready to chase me out of town for being a miserable healer. She looked more torn than angry.

Had I misjudged her? Was it possible she wasn't here to berate me? Something had made her approach me today, and I bit my lip to hold in a babble of questions and demands that might scare her off.

"You have proven yourself twice, Healer, and perhaps you've even earned the honorific this pup has been claiming. It's been centuries since we've known a true guardian."

I twitched as if she'd poked me. Oliver had started calling me *guardian* after I'd saved the marmot and a half dozen other gargoyles Elsa's invention had ensnared while it'd been tearing up the park. I hadn't put much stock in it. He was young and worshipful, and working with *Guardian Mika* sounded more impressive than *Healer Mika*. I hadn't realized the title meant anything, but the gryphon implied it did.

"If I'm going to trust you . . ." She pivoted on a hind foot and paced away from me and back, tail lashing. "If I'm going to save you . . ." She paused to peer into Rourke's faded eyes. With a choked roar, she spun away and thrust her beak so close to Oliver's snout that their breaths mingled. My brave companion didn't flinch.

The gryphon's voice rumbled with anguish when she asked, "Is she really a guardian? Is she worthy?"

"My life is hers," Oliver said.

"You are too young to know what you say."

Oliver quivered, wings flaring in anger. "I've held her spirit inside me. My age doesn't matter. I felt her in my heart. I know Mika is a guardian."

I shuddered at the reminder. I'd once transplanted pieces of my spirit into Oliver and his four siblings in a colossally stupid maneuver that would have shredded my brain if it hadn't worked. At the time, it'd been the only option I could use to save the gargoyles from being ripped apart by Elsa's invention, and I hadn't fully considered the ramifications. Nor had I realized Oliver had been able to glean anything from that piece of me, let alone that it was what convinced him I was a guardian.

I was beginning to suspect the title of *guardian* was more than an honorific, too.

The gryphon broke off her staring match with Oliver and straightened to turn her piercing regard upon me. I did my best not to fidget, but my bubbling hope made it difficult. If I guessed correctly, she knew what could save the marmot—what could save all the dormant gargoyles—and she seemed to be talking herself into telling me. I hunted for the right words to convince her I deserved her trust, but the longer I looked into her glowing amethyst eyes, the more certain I became that nothing I could say would be enough. Either she believed me worthy or she didn't.

I crossed my fingers behind my back.

"Guardian." The gryphon paused as if testing the word. "My name is Celeste, and I place the lives of all gargoyles into your hands with what I am about to tell you."

ABOUT THE AUTHOR

REBECCA CHASTAIN is a feminist, animal advocate, and nature devotee. She believes empathy is a hero's trait and love is a motive, an inside job, and a transformative energy that shapes each person's world. She is the *USA Today* best-selling author of the Gargoyle Guardian Chronicles series, the Terra Haven Chronicles series, and the Madison Fox urban fantasy series, among other works.

If given the opportunity, Rebecca will befriend your cat.

**Visit RebeccaChastain.com
for free stories, bonus materials, updates, and so much
more!**

FROM *USA TODAY*
BESTSELLING AUTHOR
REBECCA CHASTAIN

**Madison's new job would be perfect,
if not for all the creatures trying to
eat her soul...**

A FISTFUL OF EVIL
A FISTFUL OF FIRE
A FISTFUL OF FROST

PRAISE FOR THE MADISON FOX NOVELS

RebeccaChastain.com

Printed in Dunstable, United Kingdom

71024501R00112